I0588722

Home for Christmas

HOME *for* Christmas

A CHRISTMAS NOVELLA

Jessica Greyson

BLAINE, MINNESOTA

Home for Christmas
All rights reserved by Jessica Greyson © 2024
Published by Ready Writer Press, Blaine, Minnesota
ISBN 978-0-9884614-3-7

Cover art by Ellie Tran
Cover Design by Greyson Graphics
Interior Design by Valerie Anne Bost

Any similarities or likeness to anyone living or dead is coincidental and unintentional on the author's part, except for the naming nod to historical figures from long ago in the spirit of Mark Twain's original book which is in the public domain.

All rights reserved. No part of this publication may be reproduced, stored in a retrieval system, or transmitted in any form or by any means—electronic, mechanical, photocopying, recording, or otherwise—without prior written authorization from the author. The only exception is brief quotations in written reviews. Furthermore, this work may not be processed by or used to train artificial intelligence systems without the explicit, written consent of the author.

24 25 26 27 28 39 30 31 32 33   10 9 8 7 6 5 4 3 2 1

Dedication

For those who seek the light,
and those who kindle it.

Mhmm! That smells good! Please tell me that you are cooking because you got good news," said Bethany as she dropped her backpack and flopped onto the couch which had been Tacey's bed for the last two weeks.

Tacey appeared from the kitchen with an apron tied around her waist.

"Not yet."

"People are silly for not hiring you, you know."

"I had an interview at the coffee shop, and think I'll hear back from them, but they said they'd call in a week."

Bethany rolled her eyes."Why can't they just hire you on the spot?"

"They need to check my references."

"References-shemfrences!"

"All I need is someone to give me a chance! I know I'd do a good job, but with no work experience in a place like New York City . . ."

Bethany sat down at the laptop that Tacey had left open, perusing the tabs."You're applying to all of these?

A timer went off in the closet of space they called"the kitchen."

"Trying to!" answered Tacey as she ran back into the tiny space.

"There must be something. Have you checked Craigslist?"

"Craigslist . . . Remember that killer, though?" answered Tacey from the kitchen, banging the teeny oven door shut.

"Come on; not everyone on there is a killer, or crazy. Craigslist would have been shut down if that had been the case!"

"Maybe I should update my nanny profile page again?"

"No! That last mom that interviewed you was an absolute nightmare. She wanted you to be mother, father, brother, sister, grandmother, aunt, uncle and best friend to that child, *plus* teacher, on a salary that would starve a church mouse. And she was wondering why she couldn't find someone."

"The kid was cute."

"He was a diabolical minion in training! You are too nice."

"There's no such thing as too nice."

"*We* basically grew up with a woman who acted as if she was Miss Hannigan in *Little Orphan Annie!*"

"*We* did not."

Bethany gave her a look that said *Well I don't know where you were because I grew up with Mrs Hannigan.*"Look, I got lucky: I got adopted. You continued to live with *that* awful witch of a woman, did she ever help you or do anything nice? No! She had a farewell party for you the evening before your 18th birthday and kicked you out at midnight!"

"She had a rough life."

"*You've* had a rough life."

"And I am making your life rough by sleeping on your couch and eating you out of house and home."

"Seriously, if groceries for two is the price of a personal chef, I'll take it! You spoil me. Besides, you don't think I want my best friend living on the streets, now, do you?"

"Sometimes I think it's just too much—"

"Stop it, Tacey! Besides, my parents said you can stay until the cows come home, as far as they care. And since we don't have cows, they aren't ever coming home, so that means you can stay forever."

"That is asking too much of anyone."

"Is it? I like having you around."

"Me around? What for?"

"Did I mention the personal chef who cooks gluten free for me? Have you tried for a cooking job?"

"McBurgers, but they aren't hiring anyone who isn't bilingual."

"Oh! Look at this! It says '*Are you my look alike? If you are it could get you . . .* ' and it just has dollar signs; *lots* of them."

"It sounds scammy."

"Hmmm . . . maybe. But it sounds interesting. Oh! Girl! How tall are you?"

"Five feet eight inches, and a quarter."

"Tall people hanging those quarter inches over us short people who only see their armpits because they can only scrape five two with heels on. I am barely tall enough to go on rollercoasters."

"Well, at least it's exact!" laughed Tacey.

"What size do you wear?"

"I don't know. Whatever fits from the thrift store, I think I have everything from a small to a sixteen."

"Beauty standards at their finest. I am waiting for the day they put 'one size fits all' on every size and create a *Hunger Games* fashion melee."

"Ugh! That book is too violent."

"Still haven't read it?"

"No."

"Hmmm. Just as well, I guess."

"Do you want water or soda with your pizza?"

"Oh, soda."

"Coming right up, with Italian dressing on your salad."

"Only, ever and always," answered Bethany as she typed madly on the laptop.

Tacey brought out a big bowl of salad in one hand and a large tray of pizza in the other. Going back to cupboard of the kitchen she brought out glasses filled with ice and a two-liter of soda.

"You got us *Tahitian Treat,* huh? I haven't had that in ages." said Bethany glancing up from her typing.

"It was on sale."

"And Pepsi wasn't?"

"Nope." Tacey poured some of the pink-red bubbling beverage into both glasses."Remember how we used to call it Jungle Soda, and pretend to have adventures on that little island with this as the only thing to keep us alive?"

"We knew so little about survival skills back then, I don't know if they are any better now. Honestly, I didn't know Tahiti was even a place until, like, four years ago."

"Is that what it's named after?"

"Yup. Tahiti: an island of grandeur and beauty. At least, that is what google said."

"What are you doing?" asked Tacey."You look like you're typing for your life."

Bethany hit the touchpad and smiled."Getting you a job!"

"Not that one with all the dollar signs!"

"It can't hurt. People get discovered like that all the time!"

"People get trafficked and *murdered* like that!"

"Well, you don't have to answer it if you don't want to. But it can't hurt, and it sounded interesting. Besides, taking a risk on a big job could be more profitable than flipping a year's worth of burgers!"

"I won't be a match. There is no way I look like some internet stranger, I don't even know who my family is, how could I resemble anyone?"

"Are you sure? You could be this woman's doppelganger! Or find out that she is your long-lost identical twin sister!"

"Come on! This isn't the *Parent Trap*! Besides, why would a reasonable adult want a twin?"

"Split an inheritance?"

"More like escape murder charges or creditors."

"Your mind is really dark this evening!"

"I am just saying! There is good and bad, and I would rather get something secure. If only seasonal jobs were hiring, things would be okay. But having a birthday right before Thanksgiving and not realizing that you're about to be kicked out of house and home without notice stinks, everyone has finished hiring for the season." and Tacey sighed, kicking the table leg. Shel felt raw, even though she tried to make light of it to Bethany.

"That's why you have me!"

"Yes, and I'm so grateful I do!"

"What do you say to eating this pizza and then watching a movie before bed?"

"That sounds good. What do you want to watch?"

"*A Christmas Carol*, Muppets edition."

"What?"

"You really missed out on all of the good classics!"

"Or brain numbing childishness!"

Bethany shrugged."It is all the brain power I have for tonight. Now let us bless this food and eat. I am starving!"

The movie had played halfway through before Bethany fell asleep. Tacey pulled a blanket over her exhausted friend's shoulders and moved back to the dining room table. Sitting down she slipped in earbuds and turned Christmas carols on her laptop to drown out the Muppets' antics on screen.

Time to finish filling out these applications—most of which I'll probably never hear back from. Oh, God! I need help. I don't know what to do or where to go. I am grateful for the kindness of my friends, but I don't know how to make this work. I used to think being a kid was hard, but being an adult is so much harder. I need help, but I don't even know where to start. I know Bethany would give me her right arm if she had to, but I don't want to be a burden. I wonder if this is how Mary and Joseph felt, knocking on all the inn doors only to be turned away. I need something. Anything! I'd even take a stable! Something that is stable . . . she sighed and smiled at her lame joke. *Ugh I am so tired I am going crazy or something. Maybe it was the Tahitian Treat, or the Muppets?* She glanced over the tabs pulled up on her screen to glare at the parading puppets singing and dancing in the next room.

A notification from Skype appeared on the screen.

Edwina Troubador would like to chat.

Edwina? Who is Edwina?

Tacey clicked the notification. *It is probably clickbait. I'll just block them, so they don't bug me all night.*

Edwina: I can't believe you look like me. You are my lookalike! Can you do a video chat? Please!? I really need this!!

Clicking on Edwina's profile picture, she tried to get a better idea of who was messaging her. It was a black and white silhouette against a window overlooking the New York skyline.

Tacey's arrow hovered over the chat box as she tried to decide what she should do.

Please!?

Taking a deep breath, Tacey paused her Christmas music and clicked the chat box.

Please God, help!

Tacey: Hi! Is this about the look-alike job on Craigslist?

A moment later the video call screen popped up. The red button would end the call but the green . . .

Please don't let me make a mistake! I can always hang up . . .

Moving the arrow over the green button, she pressed it to answer.

Shock rippled through her and she jumped as a girl who looked just like her stared at her through the computer screen. Granted, she had slightly different hair and eye color but she felt as if she was looking into a mirror.

"What?" gasped Tacey, breathless.

"I know, right!?" Even the voice was familiar, it was like hearing an echo for words she hadn't said."I saw your face and thought you were joking. Seriously! I was hoping for a doppelgänger, but this exceeds all my hopes. I need you for this job! So badly! You have no idea."

"Okay?" Tacey felt herself tingling with shock. She was struggling to keep up with this person who looked nearly like a twin. The longing for family and familiarity swelled with an unfulfilled longing that had gripped her since *that* day

"So, I know I didn't put much on the craigslist ad because, well, whatever. Listen, I am a hard-studying law student who desperately needs some R&R, and I've only got Christmas break in which to get it, *and* I can't handle family drama right now. So, I essentially need you to take my place at a dining room table for two weeks. My family is so busy and so crazy, they won't even notice it's not me."

"What? But Christmas is for family . . ."

"But you're an orphan. Why would that matter to you?"

"What? How did you know?"

"I did a rush background check and got the lowdown. *You* don't have anyone for Christmas, and I have too many. We will essentially swap places! Except I'm going to Tahiti. No one will notice. I've prepared a folder with my family's holiday schedule and all the family members that you'll need to know, I'll email that to you. You'll hardly have to say or do anything! Just be disgruntled and scroll on your phone no one will care."

"I-I am not sure if—"

"I know it sounds like a lot. Could I meet you in person tomorrow and give you the lowdown?"

"And how—how much are you . . . ?"

"Oh! How of thoughtless of me! $5,000."

"$5,000?!" whispered Tacey, astounded at the amount.

"If it is not enough, I can do more. Say, $7,000? Look—I am desperate, and that $500 a day; you are practically a movie star! You'd get half up front, in cash, when we make the switch if you decide that you're up for it, and the rest when I get home from my trip. What do you say? Wanna give it a go?"

"I guess."

"Incredible! You can't believe how thrilled I am! I'll send you the time and the location for the meet-up tomorrow and we can finish all the details in person. Bye!"

The screen blinked black, and Skype popped up with a survey asking how the call was. Tacey tapped the five stars and then sat there in the dark for several moments trying to grasp exactly what had happened. She wanted to stand up and dance, or to squeal, and yet part of her felt as if she was gasping in shock. She pressed play to her Christmas music again, drowning out the Muppet's dialogue.

This moment called for celebration, and yet, perhaps, not quite yet. She would still have to wait to see if she actually got the job. *She said she'd be sending an email, didn't she?*

Opening the email tab on her computer, she pressed refreshed to see if anything had come in.

A message appeared.

She clicked on it.

Meet me tomorrow Blue Box Café. 12 o'clock sharp. I've made reservations under my name: Edwina Troubadour. Please start looking through the folder I've attached. I will have a hard copy with me tomorrow for you to study and memorize to the best of your ability.

Tacey clicked on the file and it started downloading a zipped folder.

When it finally finished downloading, she scanned it for viruses, just in case. It came back clean. Taking a deep breath, she right-clicked the file and found the unzip folder button, changed the destination to desktop. She created a new folder and named it *BIG JOB*.

Once the files transferred, she opened the folder and began to read.

There were various files: Events, Makeup, Wardrobe, Family, People You Should Know, Routine, House floor plans, Shopping List, Pictures.

I wonder what her family is like? She opened that document.

The first thing she saw was a man's face with the title *Dad*. Next to the picture was stated his job, net worth, business associates, hours of usual work, and his website.

Every family member was listed, with their credentials, as if they were work resumes.

Mom.

Uncle.

Aunt.

Cousins.

Grandmother.

Tacey gazed at their faces and browsed what she could see of their world. *How can Edwina not want to spend time with these people? They are her family! They are hers . . . and yet she doesn't want to be around them. It's so sad! She doesn't know how good she has it. She actually has people.*

She became absorbed in the world that was Edwina Troubadour's.

As the music from the DVD credits began to play, Bethany roused herself with a tired moan."Oh! I slept through the best parts. Ugh, I am dead tired. Night . . ." she mumbled, stumbling off to her room and closing the door behind her. Tacey wanted to call out after her that she had an interview, but keeping Bethany from a decent night's sleep when she obviously needed it didn't seem like the best idea. I'll tell her tomorrow after the interview, if I get the job. There will be so much to tell her and to surprise her with! Joy rippled through her, leaving her breathless with anticipation. I'll be able to make my own money, and with it I can establish myself and get my feet under me, and maybe even go to college! But what do I want to study? Or maybe I'll just get another job. She sighed. And, maybe, someday, I'll meet someone, and we'll have a family together. My own family, where we will always be home for Christmas! But, just for once, I'll be in a home for Christmas. A real home. It won't be mine, but it will be *home.*

*M*edical discharge.

Miles sighed, and slipped the papers into the front pocket of this duffle bag,

I barely made it three years into my enlistment and I've spent months getting better from a training accident only to have them say that I'm not fit for service anymore. At least Mom will be happy, though goodness only knows what I'm going to do after this.

It was not what he had been hoping for, but it was true he was not fit for military service—at least, not in the position he had been working towards. He had been given the option of a desk job, but he had turned it down. His mom had been begging him to come home ever since he had enlisted, telling him there would be a position waiting for him in his"Dad's" company. *I was in my Dad's company.* He thought remorsefully

"Hey! At least you get to go home for Christmas!" Daniel said, sprawling out on the bunk next to his.

"I think—" he sighed letting the sentence die unfinished. *It's never been the same since Dad left.*"I've just been avoiding Christmas for years."

"Yeah, that's what you've been telling me this whole time. Why though? It is Christmas in the Hamptons! People would *kill* to be in your shoes!"

"You wouldn't want to take this bullet for me?"

"Nah. If I took your shoes, I couldn't date your sister."

"You think you have a chance with Edwina?"

"No . . . but she did accept my friend request on Facebook, at least!"

"Did she really, now?"

"Yeah, she did. She even likes some of my photos sometimes."

"Really?"

"Yup!"

"That is more than she does for me."

"Is she really that rotten?"

"To the core."

"Come on cheer up Miles. Spoiled or not she is still your sister.

"Stepsister," Miles corrected.

"Okay so think of the good things. Like in a few hours you'll be at smashing parties! Forgetting all of us poor souls who have sold our souls to the government."

"I could never forget all of you. Besides all of these partiers will see me as charity case: lost, troubled and in need of guidance. Or want me to invest thousands to millions of dollars I don't have."

"Have you told them you're coming home for Christmas yet?"

"No, I figured that would be my surprise. I'll get a taxi or an uber from the airport, or something."

"Well, do tell Edwina I said hello."

"If she'll speak to me, I certainly will."

"You two are like sworn foes! I don't know why your parents haven't told you guys to grow up yet."

"They've tried! I'd be willing to call it off if Edwina would."

"You're older than she is; you should call it off first."

"I've tried, but she won't let the torch die. Seriously, that woman is going to make an insane lawyer when she gets her degree. She'll hunt down evidence like no other. I would hate to be in a case against her."

Daniel laughed. "Well, in that *case*, if I ever get in trouble, I'll make sure to hire her."

Miles laughed mildly at Daniel's attempt at humor.

"Twenty-four hours and I'll be home for Christmas."

CHAPTER

Four

t was late when Tacey crawled onto the couch. She had studied and studied the notes that Edwina had sent her. It all seemed terrifying, but at the same time, so incredible. *If I can only pull this off . . .*

Setting her alarm so that she wouldn't be late, she went to sleep.

Grey light streamed in through the large bay window over the back of the couch, and Tacey blinked several times at the snow falling in great big flakes before she rolled over on the couch to look at the time on her cellphone.

10:45 stared at her in large red numbers.

"No! No! No! How!? Oh no!!"

Rushing to the closet in Bethany's room where her interview outfit was hanging, she changed quickly. Stopping in the bathroom briefly to brush her teeth and her hair, she tossed makeup into her purse, threw on her coat and second-hand boots, and rushed out the door—catching the subway just in time, it was a miracle. Standing with her arm wrapped around a subway pole, she dug in her purse for the mascara, eyeliner, blush, and lipstick that Bethany had helped her purchase to make her look more professional for interviews. She knew the route she had to take, and if all went well, she would be only a few minutes late.

As they were coasting into the first station, the train slammed its breaks unexpectedly. The liquid eyeliner Tacey was applying made a dramatic upward detour across her eyelid, through her eyebrow, and onto her forehead.

"No, no, no!" she exclaimed. Capping the eyeliner, she shoved it back into her purse and tried to rub away the damage it had caused. It spread.

"Honey," said a woman seated near her,"What exactly are you doing?"

"My makeup . . . ?"

"I can see that! What are you trying to do it for?"

"A job interview."

"Ah nah honey; you come sit yourself down right here and let Latisha do your makeup!" the woman commanded giving the man next to her a pointed look. The man moved and Tacey hesitantly sat in the newly opened seat, sending the man an apologetic look.

"Now how long does Latisha have?"

"Until 5th Avenue."

"Oh, honey! Latisha had better get down to business!" The woman whipped out not one but two bags of makeup and rummaged through them before unfolding a set of brushes wrapped up for safe keeping. The woman opened various bottles of liquid, swept pallets and then her face with a deft hand wielding her large and tiny brushes that spoke of year of experience. Taking combs and hair spray, Latisha managed Tacey's hair in a few competent strokes, pulling it back with a barrette, then spraying so it would stay in place. Latisha handed Tacey a mirror."Now tell me what you think honey."

Tacey looked into the mirror and her jaw dropped."I almost don't look like me, but I also look more like me."

Latisha laughed."That's good makeup for you! Now take this: here are a few makeup samples. I have a feeling you'll need them," she said, handing her a little bag with small sample items tucked inside."Oh! And for good measure—" the woman pulled out a tiny tube of something,"—can you wear perfume?"

"I don't know; but I didn't have time to shower this morning," Tacey replied.

Latisha placed it in her hand."Apply this, when you get out of the subway, to your wrists, then dab them behind your ears." Then she added under her breath,"And apply some as deodorant *if* you need it."

"How can I ever thank you!? Can I pay you? You have done so much for me!"

Latisha laughed."Lord, child, no! Now go this is your stop."

"Thank you for being my guardian angel and fairy god-mother all in one. I feel like I'm going to a ball!"

"Well, go get that job!"

"I will!" Tacey called over her shoulder as she rushed out the subway doors and into the moving mob of people, clutching her purse in one hand and the gifts from Latisha in the other. She bounded up the stairs and onto the slushy 5th Avenue sidewalk. Central Park across the road was covered in snow. It looked perfect for a romantic stroll through a winter wonderland—that was, if one had someone to romantically stroll with. She rushed down the street until she reached what she was looking for: Tiffany's. The Blue Box Café was on the third floor, and she was going to be a few minutes late—but first she needed to find a restroom to apply the perfume that Latisha had given her.

The small bottle was an opaque, white-labeled *Soprano* by Fleur de Lys. It smelled sweet and almost woodsy, but not overbearing. It was somehow magical and feminine, as if it was something a wood nymph in one of *Anne of Green Gables* stories would bedeck herself in before going to see the fairy queen at the dryad's bubble.

Prancing up the stairs to the classical orchestration of Jingle Bells that played through Tiffany's, Tacey arrived at the doors of the Blue Box Café.

"I am here to meet Miss Edwina Troubadour, please."

"She hasn't arrived yet, but her table is ready, This way, if you please, miss," said a waiter, leading her to an empty table. He pulled out her chair, Tacey sat down. *Is this what it feels like to be a princess?*

"Can I get something for you to drink? Water, tea, coffee?"

"Water is fine with me."

The man nodded and turned away.

Tacey sat, taking in the view around her and people-watching. Everything was decorated in "Tiffany blue," accented with white and touch of elegant evergreen for Christmas.

Oh . . . it is so beautiful.

The waiter brought her a glass of water and sat it in front of her.

"Anything else, miss?"

"No, not at the moment. Thank you."

Taking a sip of the water, Tacey took a deep breath. She was starting to feel anxious. *What if Edwina doesn't show up? What will I need to do? Will I need to order something? How much does food cost here?* She glanced through the menu and grimaced. *Everything here is so expensive! Maybe, I should take a selfie and send it to Bethany, and tell her I am here for a job interview . . .*

She slipped out her hand-me-down, cracked-screen, off-brand smart phone and took a shy selfie with the menu. She had just pulled up a text message box when there was a rush beside her.

"Oh my! Traffic was crazy this morning!" complained a newly familiar feminine voice beside her as a large file folder landed on the table.

Tacey jumped slightly and looked up to see her newly discovered doppelgänger looking back at her. In real life she could see the slight differences—Edwina's eyes were green, and her hair darker than Tacey's copper brown locks—but the resemblance was decidedly uncanny. It had been strange on the computer screen last night, but in person it was even more unreal.

A broad smile crossed the other girl's face as she slid into the chair across the table.

"I can hardly believe this! Oh my! You're so perfect for the job! Did you have time to go over the files I sent you last night?"

"Yes, I studied them for quite a while."

"Well, let's see how well you did," Edwina said, pulling photographs out of the folder."Who is this?"

"Your father," Tacey answered promptly.

"Ahem! Who is he to *you?*" Edwina asked pointedly.

"Oh!" Tacey blushed."Dad."

"Exactly!"

Edwina whipped through the rest of the photographs and Tacey was pleased that she only fumbled over a few of the names.

"You did really well, but I also have these prepared for you to study," Edwina said, tapping a binder she had dropped on the folder.

Tacey flipped the binder open to find each photo and bio in a sheet protector.

"You've done a lot of preparation to do this."

"Not really; I hired a temporary personal assistant to put it together for me. I've been planning on going to Tahiti for months, but my stepmother who you will call Mom—" Edwina rolled her eyes dramatically"—kept insisting that I come home for Christmas and completely ignored my suggestions that we should take a family vacay instead! I mean, we could all really use it, and Tahiti is gorgeous!"

Tacey refrained from asking about what Edwina's father thought about the entire thing.

"In my opinion, Christmas is just a commercial holiday rigged with social bombs waiting to go off and unneeded family obligations during a time when I could be getting much-needed R&R in Tahiti, reading a book and basking in the sun. I need to get out of New York, and snow, and obligations, and cities, just for a few days! The woman would understand that if she had ever gotten a college degree . . . but did she? no! Ugh! Seriously! . . . But back to the subject at hand. You have studied what I sent you last night and you have the people down, but you also have to wear the right things. I have all my outfits planned for each outing and I have set out my makeup for you so it should be easy to follow; don't screw it up!"

Tacey nodded, and Edwina unexpectedly grabbed her hands."Have you ever had a manicure?"

"No . . ."

"No matter. I have an appointment for one right after this, also a hair appointment. We will have to get your hair darkened. And we'll have to get you contacts so our eyes will the same color—you won't have a problem wearing color contacts, will you?"

"I don't think so."

"Good. Do you have any questions?"

Tacey paged through the binder once again, feeling like she should have questions to ask but unsure what they would be . . . other than the one that lurked like a giant elephant in her mind.

"Are you sure your family won't mind?"

"Mind? They'll just be happy I'm there in body!" Edwina laughed brightly."Seriously, you likely won't even have to talk to anyone."

Tacey took a deep breath.

"Well, if you're ready to sign the agreement, we're good to go."

"I think so."

"Perfect! Read through this and sign, and then I'll explain some perks of being me for two weeks."

Tacey carefully read through the agreement and signed with the pen offered to her.

"Don't forget that this is a legally binding contract. If you break any of these rules, or don't fulfill your obligations, I can sue to you to death's doorstep," said Edwina.

I wish you would have said that before I signed—I might have not agreed. Tacey winced internally.

"All right! Now for some goodies that come with being Edwina Troubadour," Edwina said, pulling out a small bag and handing it to Tacey.

Tacey took it hesitantly.

"These are things you'll get to keep once you go home— well, except for the credit card; that you'll have to be super careful with."

Tacey pulled out the tissue paper to discover a wallet. Inside was a copycat license of Edwina's, a credit card, and the initial job payment in beautiful crisp hundred-dollar bills. She almost started crying. It was more money than she had seen in her entire life.

"Keep going—that's not all," prodded Edwina.

Pushing more tissue paper aside, she discovered an iPhone box and accessories.

"What? Are you sure?"

"Yes, it's the latest iPhone. It's exactly like mine, case and all. I've already put all of the necessary contacts in it. I wouldn't do anything too personal on it, like text your real friends or something like that. Also, be really careful about what music you listen to. I've uploaded all of my music on there, so try and stay close to that, just in case!"

"I won't," Tacey promised, *At least, I'll do my absolute best not to.*

"You ready to go get that manicure?" Edwina squealed.

"Yes, I think so."

"Fabulous!"

Five

The afternoon had been a complete whirlwind—manicure, pedicure, hair appointment, plus figuring out how to insert the troublesome contacts—so that she looked just like Edwina. They had gone on a shopping spree to find her a"going home" outfit for that evening, and now it was hanging on the bathroom shower curtain rod. Everything was set for Edwina's flight to Tahiti at 10:00 P.M., while she, little Tacey Canty, would be headed off to a luxury home in the Hamptons by 7:00, with the plan being for her to meet Edwina and her friends at the airport so that she could take the car directly back to Edwina's home. While Edwina was going out to dinner with friends, she had slipped back home to prepare.

Tacey texted Bethany the picture she had taken before the interview.

Guess what Beth!? I got the job! It's crazy! I start tonight. I love you! I'll catch up soon.

Bethany didn't reply.

She's probably studying for exams.

Tacey admired the crushed velvet gown hanging on the shower rod and looked at the price tag again. According to Edwina it was a knockoff of the dress Edwina was wearing that night, but to Tacey, that price tag did not look like a knock off—it was more than she'd paid for her clothes for an entire year. She had always shopped for clothes at secondhand stores, and all of this was a bit more excessive than she had anticipated. *I could buy groceries for a few weeks with what she paid for this dress.* Taking in the time, she realized she barely had any to get ready. She had to shed all signs of Tacey Canty and prepare to step out the door as Edwina Troubadour, heiress and future lawyer. Her nails were perfectly manicured and made beautiful little tapping nail sounds. With her makeup freshly done by an expert and her hair darkened, she hardly knew her own reflection.

Unzipping the back, she shed Tacey Canty, and slipped on Edwina Troubadour. Looking in the mirror Tacey laughed.

"I can hardly believe it's me!" She pinched herself."Ow! It is me! I wish Bethany was here to see this!"

Taking out her fancy new phone, she snapped a picture and sent it to her old phone, to send it to Bethany.

Pulling out a few crisp hundred dollar bills, she set them out with a note for Bethany on the table.

I got the job! Thank you so much! I'll see you after Christmas! I love you! -Tacey

Her old phone buzzed with the text from her new phone, so she forwarded the photo to Bethany with a text: *Off to work. I'll see you soon. Love you!*

She slipped her old phone and its charger into her new purse's secret zipper pocket, placed the wallet and phone in the main pocket, pulled on her new coat and shoes and walked out the door.

She arrived at the airport and stood waiting just inside the door where Edwina had said to meet them. She was early, but she needed this time to calm her nerves and run over the last few details of her mission. People treated her differently—instead of seeing a scrawny girl in second-hand clothing, they saw a manicured young lady *I didn't realize how much people looked on the outside and not the inside. Oh God, give me eyes to see people's hearts, and not what they wear.*

Her phone buzzed: it was Edwina. *Be there in a minute. Meet me at the curb and we'll swap.*

Tacey stepped out to the airport curb and watched as a limo pulled up. All four girls piled out, and one shrieked when she saw her.

"Edwina! Oh my! You didn't tell us! You've done wonders! I wish I had thought of the same thing to get *my* mother off *my* back!"

Edwina glided out after her four friends."I know! Isn't she just darling? Now Tacey, you know exactly what to do?

Driver," said Edwina, turning sharply to the man who was taking piece after piece of luggage out of the trunk. "You'll be taking *this* Edwina home for me; not a word—remember the bonus."

"Yes, miss," he said, placing the last piece of luggage on the sidewalk.

Tacey slid into the limousine and the driver closed the door behind her. There were various kinds of food and drink in the back.

"Help yourself to anything they left," said the driver as he got in and pulled into traffic. "I think she ordered you a meal in one of the styrofoam boxes. If she didn't, we can stop anywhere you'd like to eat."

Tacey opened a box with *Edwina the II* marked on top and discovered a salad topped with chicken and fruit.

"I found something, thank you! Do you need anything to eat?"

"No, I am good, miss."

Tacey closed her eyes, bowed her head, and thanked God for the meal and job.

They drove through New York and at last arrived at the beautiful Hamptons. Driving past the fancy houses made her feel like Cinderella, passing a thousand fine estates on her way to the palace. *I can't believe that I am doing this! . . . Why am I doing this?! Oh God, please keep me out of trouble.*

The limo stopped before one especially grand house, and the driver got out and opened her door. "The side door has been locked tight for the night. You will have to use the front door to get in."

"Thank you so much!"

"Not a problem. Good luck," he said with a tip of his hat as he drove off.

Tacey felt like a criminal sneaking up to the house. She clutched her keys tightly to her chest. *Now to slip inside, upstairs, and into Edwina's room.* She felt like she would be better able to grasp what was going on from there—and hopefully she would not have to face anyone until tomorrow morning, after she had gotten her bearings. *I can't wait to kick off these heels; that should have been on the list of things you should know how to do. Walk gracefully in high heels*

Just as she reached the steps, someone shouted behind her.

"Edwina!"

She whirled to look behind her and saw a man coming in the gate.

Tacey hadn't realized just how slippery the sidewalk was until she lost her footing . . . she was struggling to regain it . . . she was falling . . .

Everything went black.

CHAPTER

Six

"Thanks!" he said to the taxi driver as he paid and stepped out of the bright yellow vehicle onto the slippery sidewalk, lugging his duffle bag.

He had started to walk leisurely up the front walk when he caught sight of a lithe figure on the stairs.

"Edwina!" he called out. *She'll probably hiss at me like a feral cat.*

The girl whirled around in surprise. Her feet flew out from underneath her and her hands flailed in the air before she hit the cement with a hard thump.

He raced forward and knelt beside her.

"Edwina? Edwina?" He shook her gently.

Her eyes fluttered open and she looked at him, dazed.

"Edwina, are you okay?" *Why did I ask her that? She probably has a concussion.*

She looked at him groggily."Edwina? I'm not Edwina—I'm, I'm . . . Ta . . ." She sounded drunk. Abruptly she asked,"Who are you?"

She must be drunk, if she can't remember me—unless she really has erased me from her mind."I'm Miles, your *beloved* stepbrother." He said with a sarcastic undertone.

"Miles? I don't have a brother . . ." Her hands went to her temples.

He choked out a laugh; to have Edwina say these things to his face stung bitterly, even he knew she had felt them for years. She resented him; they had never gotten along. *Well, at least you're honest.*"You've had a concussion, and maybe too much to drink. Think you can get up?"

"Why am I on the ground? What happened? Everything hurts! I am so cold," she whimpered.

"Come, I'll help you up."

He offered her his hand, and she tried to get up, but her heels slipped again on the ice and she slid back to the ground."Ow! I hate these shoes!"

He couldn't help his laugh. *First common sense you have had in years.*

"It's not funny. Everything hurts."

"I am sure it does. Now come on. Let's try again."

Leaning over, he scooped his sister into his arms. She let out a small shriek and clung to his neck, looking into his face with wonder.

After walking up the steps, he set her on her feet and pressed the doorbell. Oddly, she still clung to him. She seemed to be struggling to stand steadily in her heels after the concussion.

After several moments there was the sound of movement from inside, the familiar click of shoes and his mother opened the door.

"Merry Christmas!" he exclaimed.

"Miles!" The joy in his mother's tone did his heart good. She plunged into his arms with a sob, nearly knocking Edwina over in her excitement. "You're home! You're home."

"And home to stay," he added softly.

He glanced over at Edwina, who looked as if she was ready to topple over. She suddenly swayed and his hand reached out to grab her coat.

"Mom, I am sorry," he said, untangling himself from her embrace, "I think Edwina's had a concussion. She fell and hit her head on the sidewalk." He omitted that it was probably his fault.

His mother turned to Edwina—whom she finally saw—and was instantly brimming with concern.

"Oh honey, are you all right?"

He waited for Edwina to snap and say something nasty to her, as she had to him.

"I don't know," she whimpered instead.

"Both of you come inside. Don't stay a moment longer in this cold."

Edwina stepped forward, struggling to stay on her feet.

It's easier if I do just it. He leaned over and picked her up. She did not squeal this time, but did clasp her arms around his neck again. Her heels fell off her feet, yet she didn't offer a word of admonishment or complaint at his treatment of her expensive and usually highly-prized property.

"Come set her in the entertainment room. I'll get some ice and pain meds."

"Thanks mom," he said, walking with her towards the large room filled with plush sofas, blankets, and a larger-than-life big-screen TV.

Miles set Edwina on the couch. She fumbled to take off her jacket and he leaned down to help her remove it, revealing a lush crimson velvet evening gown underneath. He didn't wonder she was shivering—evening gowns weren't meant for warmth. Grabbing a plush mink blanket, he threw it over her.

"I am going to get my bag and your purse; tell mom I'll be back shortly."

She nodded and he went to retrieve his duffle bag from outside, but he met the maid and the butler coming in with his bag and Edwina's purse.

"I'll take this up to your room, sir," said the butler hoisting it out of his reach.

"I can manage it."

"Sir, I am sure your mother would prefer to see you."

That is right, this is what they are paid to do.

"Do you think Miss Edwina would like her purse with her? Or should I set it in her room?" asked the maid holding the luxury red bag.

Edwina is prodigiously fond of her purses. "I'd better take it to her. She'll probably want to text her friends about her little accident."

"Of course," said the maid, handing it over to him decorously.

Returning to the entertainment room he found his mom entering with ice, a bottle of pain reliever, and a glass of water.

She sat beside Edwina on the couch, and once again, not a word of censure or complaint did Edwina offer.

Has Edwina changed this much since . . . ? Or is she just that drunk? I don't understand.

Without a murmur Edwina took the pain reliever with water, and applied the icepack to the sore spot on her head.

"Thank you so much," she murmured.

After settling her more comfortably on the couch, his mom finally turned to him and gave him a relieved smile.

"I'm so glad you're home. I've missed you so much."

He smiled at her grimly.

"Want to step out and talk for a minute?" he asked. Edwina did not need to know everything that was going on; though in her current condition, she probably, did not care.

"Edwina, we are just going to step out for a minute. Call us if you need anything," said his mom patting her arm.

"Okay," she said limply, wriggling deeper under the mink blanket.

They stepped out of the entertainment room; his mom could not seem to let go of his arm.

"Oh Miles, I am so happy you're home! So happy, but are you okay?"

"I am fine, Mom—the damage—I couldn't pass the med eval to go back into full time service. They offered me a desk job but I told them you had one waiting."

His mother launched herself at him with another hug."Oh Miles! You really *have* come home. You will be a wonderful asset to our team. And you won't really be leaving the uniform; you know that, right?"

"I do, Mom."

"Well, Christmas is almost here, and everything for the holidays have already been set in motion the Charity Gala and Henry's mom will be flying over in a few days. She always did like you.

Miles smiled as he thought of the wry old woman who he had always liked, she was dry, bright, and snappy like a gingersnap.

"Why don't you take this time to rest and we'll start everything for your work after the holidays. Just enjoy being home with us for a little bit?"

"Home with you and Edwina?"

"You are both older, it has been awhile. I'm just pleased that she is here. She put up such a fuss about coming and wanted everyone to go to Tahiti for Christmas. But the flight from England to the US is already getting too long for her grandmother and flying to Tahiti would be out of the question, and the Charity Gala is tomorrow night . . ."

"Tomorrow night?"

"You'll be there, right?"

"Of course, if I can find something to wear by then."

"I'll find something for you to wear so don't worry. But I should go to bed; I have an early meeting tomorrow, and have all the last-minute details with all the speakers, caterers, and so many more people to figure out. 'Though, with Edwina's injury, I should make sure she is okay."

"Where's Henry? Couldn't he stay up with her?"

"He is already in bed; he's had some outlandish days. But you know me: I'm night owl, and I am so glad I am because otherwise I wouldn't have known about your surprise until the morning. But with Edwina's concussion, I should really keep an eye on her tonight."

"Mom, why don't you get some sleep? Don't worry about Edwina's concussion. I'll stay up with her, and we'll watch *It's a Wonderful Life* or something. That should keep us going for hours."

"Are you sure you're okay with that, darling?"

"Of course, Mom."

She leaned forward and kissed him on his cheek."It's so good to have you home."

"Yeah, I know."

"We'll talk more in the morning."

"Sounds good."

"Goodnight, son."

"'Night, Mom."

He walked her to the staircase that led upstairs before returning to the entertainment room where Edwina still sat, with a meditative look on her face—an expression he had not seen before.

"Why didn't you put a movie on?"

"I don't know," she sniffed "The remote looks complicated."

"Really?"

He picked up the remote and flicked on the TV, changing the station to a continuous Christmas channel that was playing *It's A Wonderful Life,* as he had predicted. Flopping down on his side of the long custom-designed couch, he pulled out his phone and snapped a photo of Edwina. He pulled up a text chat and attached Edwina's picture.

Hey Daniel! Edwina says hello! Or, rather, she would if she didn't have a concussion. I doubt she'd remember you right now—she certainly doesn't remember me.

Moments later Daniel texted back.

Umm . . . that's not Edwina.

A chill ran through Miles. *Ugh. He's playing you—it's just another one of his jokes. Of course it's Edwina. Who else could it be?*

Hahaha! Very funny! Stop pulling my leg.

That's not Edwina.

A moment later Daniel sent a screenshot. It was a picture of Edwina and a bunch of her friends crammed together in the back of a vehicle. The caption underneath it read "*Tahiti here I come!" followed by* a bunch of plane, palm tree, sun, and heart emojis. The time stamp said it was ten minutes old. Her phone had been outside in the cold at that time.

Are you sure? Miles fired back.

Dead sure. Want me to ping her phone?

THEN WHO IS SITTING ACROSS FROM ME??

Your guess is as good as mine.

Who did I just let into the house?

Good thing she has a concussion, so you have the upper hand if she tries to assassinate you.

I can only hope! How his fingers ached for the security of his gun! But he wasn't licensed in New York . . . yet.

The girl he had thought was Edwina reached for her purse and rummaged through it. After finding her phone, she fumbled to unlock it and seemed to be struggling to make it function.

"Are you doing okay, Edwina?"

"Yeah."

"You seem to be struggling with your phone."

"Eh, updates, you know. Make it so weird."

"Oh yeah; the latest one was a doozy."

Phone systems were updated four weeks ago—there is no way Edwina would still be struggling.

She only nodded and winced.

"Need another icepack?"

"That would be nice," she whispered.

Getting up and going to the kitchen, he got a fresh icepack from the freezer, and then grabbed a tub of ice cream, two bowls and two spoons.

The real Edwina test: she never eats ice cream, unless it's non-dairy.

Returning to the entertainment room, he was relieved to find the Edwina replacement still there.

"Do you want some ice-cream? It's *cookie-dough*."

Her eyes lit up with an expression he never saw on Edwina's face except when she spotted a *Gucci* bag.

A knot tangled in his stomach.

This young woman before him was not Edwina. He looked down into her face, looking for the subtle differences that must be there. A faint scar that had been hidden by makeup now appeared on her forehead; her chin was narrower, hair lighter, eyes—sweeter. He gulped.

This is definitely not Edwina.

"Do you want me to scoop?" she offered.

Her voice was softer than Edwina's, too. In fact, more he looked at her, the less of Edwina he saw.

"Sure," he answered, handing her the half empty ice cream container and setting the bowls down in front of her. She gave him a generous amount, and herself a tiny singular scoop.

"Don't you want more?"

She looked at him hesitatingly."Can I?"

He shrugged,"I don't see why not! Finish it off if you want. I won't have to take it back to the kitchen, then."

She smiled and spooned the rest of the pint into her bowl. Then she curled up tightly, resting her head against the icepack and holding the generous ice cream bowl.

He couldn't help but smile just a little. She was so un-Edwina-like. His phone buzzed.

So, you know George in security? He owed me a few favors. Check your email.

Oh Daniel, Daniel! what have you done now?

Opening up his emails, he found an email titled **Edwina report.** In it was her exact pinged location: John F. Kennedy

Airport. Also included was a large file called"Christmas Getaway." He opened the file and found a Craigslist ad and response, as well as detailed notes about the family, house layout, and family gathering plans. He kept scrolling in disbelief. There was also a file that contained the background report on a certain Tacey Canty, He read what was on her file.

Looks like you're stuck with Tacey for the holidays, messaged Daniel.

What am I going to do?

Does she seem like she'd kill people while they sleep?

No.

It could be fun.

It could do a lot of damage to the family if this gets out.

Always practical. He added and eye roll emoji.

Thanks for using your favor for my family.

No worries! Wouldn't want my best buddy killed on his first Christmas home in six years, you know.

Thanks! What are you doing with an Instagram account, anyway?

Getting cooking recipes, vacation ideas, and joining essential oil pyramid schemes.

Miles rolled his eyes.

Daniel, Daniel . . .

He looked over to where Edwina—*Tacey*, he inwardly corrected—was sitting, watching *It's a Wonderful Life* with all the interest of a person who had never seen it before.

Turning towards the television screen, he decided he was going to enjoy this Christmas, especially it had just gotten a lot more interesting.

*T*acey lay on the couch, eating as much ice cream as her heart desired as she watched a movie that she had only ever seen clips of before. Occasionally, she stole glances at the blond, handsome stranger sitting at the other end of the couch.

His blue eyes had stared so intensely into hers when he had asked if she was okay—not to mention that he had picked her up as if he was some romantic hero freshly fallen out of a novel. The very thought of it made her turn cherry red.

"Edwina, are you okay? Edwina? . . . Edwina?"

Oh! That's me?" Huh?"

"You're bright red."

"Oh . . . I am?"

"Yeah," he said, rising from his end of the couch and walking to her."You feeling okay?" he asked again, pressing his hand against her forehead.

She felt her blush deepen. She had never been around many boys, except those from her classes at school, and none of them had been interested in her. After school, she had never had the time for any casual social interaction with them. Her life had always been school, home, chores, cook, homework, sleep, repeat and repeat, and repeat. Therefore, most of her knowledge about males came from the books she had read, and the man towering over her was fitting the role a novelian hero, with a lithe casualness of nonchalant perfection; and she had no clue how to handle herself.

He's not on the list of people that Edwina gave to me, and she's not answering my texts. I don't know what to do with him.

That intense stare turned on her again. His blue eyes scanned her, as if he knew her true identity. Her heart quivered, and she knew that, if she was standing, her knees would be knocking together.

One capable hand cupped her chin and he looked into her eyes

Her heart skipped a beat.

"Your eyes don't seem to be dilated, unless they are equally so. Are you sure you're feeling well?"

"Yes," her voice squeaked.

A slight smile pulled at the corner of his mouth."You don't have a fever; is your stomach feeling okay? You don't feel like throwing up or anything?"

"No."

"That's good. You just had me worried with how red you were getting."

Edwina is lucky to have a brother that cares so much about her. I always wanted someone who would look out for me. How could Edwina want to miss Christmas with a family that loves her so much?

She felt the inkling of tears swelling up in her eyes so she pulled away from his hand, internally wincing."I'm fine," she whispered as she set her head down on the sofa's large cushioned arm and closed her eyes.

Her heart was stinging with pain. *How can people just leave the ones that love them this much?*

"Edwina is something hurting you?"

"I'm fine."

Slowly he moved back to the other side of the couch and Edwina tried to shut him and everything else out of her mind—everything but the story of George Bailey playing out in black and white on the screen before her.

The hour was late, and she wasn't used to staying up. She was getting tired . . . so tired. She toyed with the idea of slipping out of the room but Miles seemed to be keeping a stern eye on her.

I should have downloaded the house plan onto the phone. I don't think I can find the way to Edwina's room and that would just be awkward, since this is supposed to be my home and I should remember where my room is, even with a concussion.

She snuggled a little deeper into the leather couch under the warm mink blanket, her head cushioned on the sofa arm. Her eyes shut, and she fell asleep.

CHAPTER

Eight

He had looked deep into those eyes that were so unlike Edwina's and realized she was wearing colored contact lenses to make her eyes match his stepsister's. She certainly did not seem like the serial killer type—and it *was* like Edwina to scheme her way out of family Christmas. Tacey had blushed so hotly under his eyes, he had half wondered if a confession was on the tip of her tongue.

She's not very good at her job. I wonder if she will last all two weeks. I wonder what else Edwina changed about her looks besides the contacts to make them look more alike.

Glancing over at her, he realized she had fallen asleep. *I'll wake her in a little bit to check on her, but for now, a little nap for myself wouldn't hurt.* He leaned back into the couch and closed his eyes.

*ethany's couch is so soft I don't want to leave it.
I should get up and make her breakfast. What
time did she come in last night? This . . . doesn't
smell like Bethany's couch—it's warm and leathery and . . .*

She sat up, blinking slowly, trying to grasp her bearings.
A Christmas Carol was on the big screen television, a strange
man was sleeping soundly three cushions away, snoring quietly, and she was wearing a red crushed velvet dress.

Where am I? Memories started darting through her
mind. *That's right! Last night I fell and hurt my head—a concussion, he said? Then he called himself my brother . . . but*

Edwina doesn't have a brother—not that she put down on the documents, anyway. I should go to Edwina's room and change out of this dress into something more comfortable. Hopefully I haven't ruined it.

Slipping silently from the couch, she tip-toed out of the room on her nyloned stocking feet and into one of the grand hallways.

Where am I? I must be on the main floor which means my room is upstairs. I need to find the main hallway which is off of the living room and then leads to the dining room. No, I need to find the main entrance and staircase.

At last, Tacey found her exact location and scurried up the stairs with as much dignity as her fear would allow and found Edwina's room, which felt less like a room and more like and entire apartment. Opening the closet, she saw notes with dates pinned on each outfit.

Charity Bore

Family and Friends Dinner, several outfits were pinned with dates and details.

Christmas Eve

Christmas Morning Pajamas

Christmas Breakfast

Christmas Dinner

Is there anything comfortable here? I need to get out of this dress.

Rummaging around, she finally found a T-shirt and a pair of leggings.

Of course she's that kind of girl! Doesn't she have a pair of jeans and a flannel shirt, or even a sweatshirt? Does she wear anything comfortable, or is everything always formal? . . . I need to get these lenses out; they're making my eyes itch.

Stepping into the bathroom, she managed to get the contacts out and apply soothing eyedrops. *I'm still so tired. I wonder if I can take another nap . . . Why am I so tired?*

There was a knock on the bathroom door.

"Edwina?"

It's him! Who is he?

To avoid him she turned on the water for the jacuzzi tub before locking the door and leaning against it.

I need the phone. Where did I put it down? Did I even bring it upstairs? No, no, no! I must have left it in the entertainment room. What if he came up to bring me my purse, though? It has my phone in it, but I'd have to put in those contacts again.

She bit her lip, calculating.

Just leave me alone and the purse outside, if that is what you've come for. Also, what date is it? What am I supposed to get dressed for today? I can't go back in there—what if he's in the room because he thinks I am busy in here? What am I going to do with him? I need to take a shower; then maybe I'll feel better about what I am supposed to be doing and maybe my head will clear. Yes, a long luxurious hot bath.

Tension dripped off her shoulders and into the hot water until the water started becoming a shade of brown

"No! No! No!"

My hair! How could I forget that I'm not supposed to get my hair wet for three days? No! Now I'll need to get it recolored or something.

Climbing from the tub as quickly as possible, she dressed once in the leggings and T-shirt before stepping cautiously out into the room. The purse was sitting on the desk. Running to it, she rummaged through it and found the phone. There was one text from Edwina.

THAT IS MILES. HE IS THE ENEMY—DO NOT TALK TO HIM! Also buy him a Christmas gift. I forgot.

What? Don't talk to him? He's your brother, not your enemy. He seems really nice. But I guess I get to figure out what to get him for Christmas, now. What do you get a brother for Christmas? A watch? He had one of those. What is today?

Opening the calendar app on the phone, she looked at the date and clicked on the events.

Hairdresser appt. @ 3:30. *I've got a few hours to get there, but I just saw the hairdressers yesterday. Why do I need to see them again? Oh! Maybe they can fix the mess I made with my hair! Oh, I hope they can. It won't be so bad then.*

Charity Gala Ball

Charity Gala Ball? What? She didn't mention a ball! She said a charity event, not a ball. I won't be expected to dance, will I? What kind of dancing do you even do at a ball? Waltzing? Is that still a thing?

She rushed to the closet and pulled out the dress marked *Charity Bore.* It was most certainly a ballgown, shimmering gold with a lace up back, a small black bolero jacket and a note about where the jewelry and shoes were.

I can't dance. And I can't learn dancing in a single after-noon. They'll know for sure that I'm not Edwina. Maybe I can be sick? I'll have to be sick. Will that even work? I'll just have to pray that it will. Oh, God help me! I can't do this at all! I haven't been here for even 24 hours and already I am seriously messing this all up. I'll be in prison for impersonation before Christmas. Oh, God, I can't lose this job—please help me.

She sank down on the bed in utter exhaustion at the sheer magnitude of the stunt she was trying to pull off.

I have to do this. I just have to. I can't disappoint her, or Bethany.

Taking a deep breath, she picked up the phone and, pulling up the search bar, typed *How to Waltz.*

Several videos popped up and for the next two hours, Tacey watched, studied, and practiced the steps, listening to instructor after instructor.

I wish I had a dance partner —it would make figuring this out so much easier.

There was another knock on the door.

"Edwina?"

It was his voice again.

Tacey fumbled with the phone, trying to turn off the music and instruction, and before she could scream"no" the door swung open.

"Edwina?"

"I-I-I . . ." *I'm not supposed to talk to you . . .*

Ten

She stood in the center of the room looking con-science-stricken, something that Edwina never was.

"You're practicing. I was wondering—I haven't danced in forever. Would you give me a few pointers?" Miles

She won't fool anyone, unless I cover for her. But why should I help Edwina's cause . . . other than it makes life so much more interesting at the moment?

"Sure," she said with a shrug. "I'm feeling really clutzy after my fall last night, and I'm not sure if I'll feel well enough to go tonight, but I thought I would practice and see if I still could . . ."

He took the phone from her hand and looked through the waltz music list. After selecting a piece, he stepped in place, put his hand on her waist, and took her other hand in his. As the music started, he invited her to follow his lead with a gentle push of his finger tips into her T-shirt.

Her eyes raised to his with a look of ill-concealed wonder. *Where did Edwina find you? Well, I know on Craigslist, but how and why? And what is your story?*

The dance classes his mother had made him take were paying off. He had always had natural rhythm and once the music started, dancing was like sailing in autopilot, with Tacey following his lead.

She looks different without all of the makeup on, and her eyes are a pretty blue instead of Edwina's green. And her hair! He twirled her to see it spin out around her. There was certainly a change in hair color. It was lighter, almost coppery. The young woman in his arms was definitely not his mother's step-daughter—but he wasn't about to let on. No, it was getting far too interesting.

I wonder if she's seen Edwina's message, and how she's going to deal with it.

He had been awakened that morning by buzzing coming from the purse Tacey had left. Grabbing it, he dug through it looking for more clues as to who this Edwina-pretender really was.

The first thing he found was Edwina's phone, with one new message that obviously referred to him. However, the buzzing continued and at last he found the source: a second phone blitzing its little life away as it lit up with text message after text message.

ARE YOU OKAY?

WHAT HAPPENED TO YOU?

WHY DID YOU TAKE THE JOB???

WHAT IS GOING ON?

DON'T TELL ME THEY STOLE YOU! PLEASE ANSWER YOUR PHONE TACEY!!!

I AM SO SORRY! I SHOULD HAVE NEVER APPLIED TO THAT JOB FOR YOU!!

TACEY!!!!

TACEEEEEEEY!!!???

YOU BETTER PICK UP THE PHONE RIGHT NOW! I AM GOING CRAZY!!!

YOU DON'T LOOK LIKE YOURSELF! ARE YOU OKAY!!?

HOW DID THIS HAPPEN?

TACEEEEEEEEEEEEEEEEEEEEEEEEEEYYYYYYYYYYYYYY YYYYYYYYYYYYYYYYYY!!!!!!!!!!!!!!!

At least someone cares about her and is worried, and she didn't go into this by herself . . .

Miles turned his mind back to the present and his partner, who was now keeping her eyes glued to the ground as she followed his lead step by step.

The music paused ended as it loaded the next song on the phone.

"I think that was enough a refresher, don't you?" she said stiffly.

"Probably, though I think you've gotten a bit rusty since our dance practice days."

"School has been so busy, all I've had time to do is sit in those stiff chairs and run from class to class," she answered, not meeting his eyes.

"How are you feeling this morning, by the way?"

"Pretty okay. I am just not sure if I'll feel up for everything tonight, though," she answered, eyes still glued to the floor.

He reached for her chin, so he could look into her eyes. She tensed as their eyes met.

"Your eyes! They are—"

"Contacts!" she offered forcefully. "What do you think? I'm giving them a try, 'cause there is a guy at school. He—he likes blue eyes better."

"Then he's ridiculous," he said and looked deeply into the contact-lenseless eyes that met his.

"I don't think so, and you've been very, very rude. I think you should leave."

"I was just checking in to see how you were doing with the concussion from last night."

"I'm fine."

"Fine enough to go to the gala ball?"

"Of course. Now go!" She tried to fuss.

"Fine, fine. I am leaving."

That's the most forceful she's gotten the whole time we've been together. Finally trying to be Edwina, I see. Hmm . . . this could get better or worse. If she dances tonight like she did just now . . . Miles shook his head with a wry grin. *She needs to play the sick card, or Edwina's game will be up.*

CHAPTER
Eleven

acey watched him go, and when at last he closed the door, she let out a long, agonized sigh. *I almost didn't make it. DID I make it? He almost had me completely. AH! If I hadn't . . . I should have put the contacts in **after** I showered, but did I? No! I didn't. I should put them in now and be more careful from here on. Oh please, please, please don't let him figure it out, God. I can't lose this job! I can't! . . . I won't! I won't! Now to fix my hair. Where is the hairdresser I'm supposed to see? There isn't a location or any other details about the appointment; just a phone number. Maybe I can look the rest up from that? A* few minutes passed as she quickly googled the number. *No listings for that phone number, so maybe I should start thinking for a Christmas present for Miles. What would he like? Maybe I should look up"ideal last minute gifts for older brothers"? How am I supposed to know what he wants for Christmas? Maybe I should just ask him? Do people still do wish lists? Why don't I know any of this info? I should have asked Edwina so many more questions before agreeing to the job. How would Edwina handle this? I think she just kind of bossed people into doing what she wanted, though. Would that work—but how can you boss people when you don't know anything? That's it, I'll call the hairdresser maybe he knows something I don't.*

Switching back to the calendar, Tacey pressed the number for the hairdresser and lifted the phone to her ear. It rang and went to voicemail where a cheerful male voice greeted her ear: *Hello beautiful! I am so sorry I didn't answer—I am with another client at the moment. Once I am done making them look fabulous I'll give you call, so just leave your name after the beep—I know your number.* *beep*

Tacey struggled for words; this wasn't what she'd been expecting: a flirtatious hairdresser. Realizing she was inadvertently leaving a blank message, she fumbled with the phone and hung up. *That didn't help at all. Maybe I'll just do the best I can with my hair this evening. There has to be tutorials online how to style your hair for a ball, right? It can't be that hard.*

Taking a deep breath, she sat down and started searching YouTube for evening hairstyles tutorials. It quickly got overwhelming. By the time she set the phone down, it felt as if she had watched hundreds of videos. *How can I even pull off one of those? The videos make them look so easy, but I know that they aren't! Maybe I could just go with my hair down, or with a slight curl? Five minutes, my foot! Sure, if you've been doing your hair like that since you were in high school it might take you five minutes, but for me who has never done it, I'd be lucky if I was done in three hours! How much time do I have, anyway?*

A moment later there was a knock on the door.

"Beautiful! It's me! Time for our appointment? Can I come in?"

It was the voice from the flirtatious flamboyant voicemail.

Tacey walked over to the door and opened it. The epitome of tall, dark, and handsome was standing before her, with a large case of supplies on his arm.

"Are you ready to get glamorous?" he asked, stepping past her."Ah! This your dress. I've always admired Edwina Troubadour's taste! And now," he said, turning to face her,"let me see what she's left for me to work with."

Tacey fumbled for a reply.

"Come, sit, sit, sit! I do not have all day to create the masterpiece needed for this evening!" he said, patting the swiveling chair that sat before Edwina's boudoir.

"So, you know?" she asked, their eyes meeting in the mirror as she took the requested seat.

"Yes, she sent me a file with all the deets. I am here to make sure you match the 'Edwina look', and the rest of it is up to you. Ah! What did you do to your hair?"

"I've never had dyed hair before, and I forgot you're not supposed to wash it."

He sucked in a long breath, but then waved his hand."No matter! This is what Antonio is here for! You know this: I am the best in the biz; I will make sure you look like an Italian masterpiece!"

"I think *you're* the Italian masterpiece."

He laughed and set to work.

Within an hour he had Leondardo Da Vinci'ed her hair into a masterpiece, just as he promised.

"I left off a little makeup, since, although you may *look* like Edwina, you're not *like* her; your eyes are more innocent than hers, and to give you a dusky, dramatic look would make you look like you'd lost your soul, so I've given you a more golden look to match your dress—to match what I think might be a golden soul."

A blush rushed up her neck and into her cheeks.

"Well, I'm off to rescue the next damsel in distress! Wish me luck and be beautiful this evening. Ciao!"

"Ciao!" she echoed back as the door closed behind him.

So that is what Antonio is like! I don't think I could do that every day but he did a marvelous job. I do feel like a made-up masterpiece. Mused Tacey as she marveled at her appearance

CHAPTER

Twelve

*H*is phone buzzed.

I've arranged for the driver to have you and Edwina at the Gala by 7:00 to help greet guests. See you soon! His mom added three heart emojis.

He glanced down at his watch and did some quick math: the drive would take nearly three hours with all the pre-Christmas traffic, and it was almost 2:00 now, so they'd need to leave soon.

His phone buzzed again.

The car will be ready to pick you and Edwina up in 15 minutes.

The hairdresser was just leaving, so Miles decided to see if Edwina's replacement was ready for her grand entrance at the gala.

He had tried on the suit his mother had sent over and it had fit perfectly. He realized that the last time he had gone to this event was before he had enlisted. *I'll get to see you tonight, Dad. I wish you were here for Christmas. I still miss us as a family.* This yearly gala was dedicated, in part, to his father, since the proceeds benefitted two groups of people: people impacted by 9/11 survivors and families of victims, and people like his mother and him—

He tore his thoughts away—that wasn't where he wanted them go. *Dad, Christmas is always harder without you here.*

The promise his father had made as he left rang in Miles' head: *I'll be home by Christmas, don't you worry.* That was before a roadside bomb had taken out his father and a good portion of his unit.

War changed so much.

Now Christmas meant promises never kept.

He checked his hair one more time, straightened his red and gold-striped bowtie, and left his room.

Time to see if Edwina and her double can really pull this off.

He knocked on Edwina's door.

"Yes?" Tacey answered.

"Hurry up, Edwina! The car will be ready in a few minutes, and my mom won't want us to be late."

"I'll be there; I am just finishing with my dress!" she answered politely.

"I'll be downstairs waiting."

"Okay! Thanks!"

He shook his head at the un-Edwina-ish reply and headed down the stairs into the kitchen. He would need a snack for the long car ride. Just as he emerged the kitchen, Tacey came down the stairs.

The golden dress shimmered, her dark locks with copper undertones were half up-half down, and she looked—breathtaking. He greeted her at the bottom of the stairs.

She raised her eyes to him."Do I look all right?" A question Edwina would never have asked him.

"Perfect," he answered, something he would have never told Edwina.

She gave a little sigh of relief, and he realized—for the first time that he could remember—*they* were the ones waiting for the chauffeur. When the car pulled up, the chauffeur opened the doors and they took their seats, Tacey arranging her dress carefully so as to acquire the fewest number of wrinkles.

She pulled out her phone and started looking through what he assumed were files that Edwina had given her. Her brow knit and her mouth pursed. Biting her lower lip, she glanced up at him.

"I've been in such a tizzy all day; remind me, what is this Gala for?"

"This gala benefits families of Veterans of the war, and 9/11 survivors and their families."

"Oh." Her voice became very small and she nodded. He watched her out of the corner of his eye as she googled the gala. She was silent, but it was not like Edwina's cold"silent treatment"—this was an emotional silence; she clicked the screen of her iPhone black before sticking it into her purse and turning away to look out the car window. He thought he saw a tear slipping down her cheek.

Will she be able to fake it tonight? What will happen if she can't play the part correctly? Not only would it reveal Edwina's scheme to the family and devistate mom, but it would be a real embarrassment to the family. This is Mom's event to honor Dad's memory. I can't let Edwina ruin it, but how am I going to fix it?

His fingers tapped his leg as he tried to think of a way to keep Tacey out of the public eye. *I could lock her in a closet. . . . That's a terrible idea! I wonder if . . . ?* He pulled out his phone.

Daniel, I need help again. Tacey is going to fail as Edwina tonight. Any ideas of how to keep this from blowing up into a fiasco?

Call for a SWAT Team? Daniel messaged back.

Miles rolled his eyes. *That wasn't helpful. Thanks,* he tapped back, then rested his head against the window and thought through different scenarios, He closed his eyes.

God, please; I really need you on this one. I need to protect my family—and Edwina—and Tacey. I'm not exactly sure what to do with this all, but I need something larger than myself—or New York's SWAT team—to make this Christmas go well.

Nothing came.

Miles leaned back in the seat; he decided that he might as well enjoy the calm before the storm.

They arrived at the gala just on time. His mother met them at the door.

"I am so glad you're both here. Are you feeling okay, Edwina?"

"Much better than last night, thank you, Mom," answered Tacey.

Miles anxiously searched his mother's face for any hint of doubt as to the authenticity of the Edwina standing before her. He saw none. *But, if I did not know the truth, would I have noticed?* He tried to take a step back from the situation and see it through his mother's eyes, but his mind and body were all set for action and trouble—with Tacey being an unknown, he was in fight mode, ready to be ready at breaths notice to try and rescue the situation, especially his mother's reputation.

If he had not figured out that she was not Edwina that first evening, he would have never gone up to her room and therefore never seen her without her contacts in, and he definitely would not have checked her phone messages.

Maybe I'm just jumpy just because I know she's not Edwina.

His mother wanted to see a family that she had been trying to pull together for years finally melding. Tacey's uncharacteristic responses, to her, simply looked like a rebellious, opinionated stepdaughter who, for once, was stepping off her warpath for a Christmas truce. Miles took a deep breath— maybe tonight would not be as bad as he thought.

CHAPTER

Thirteen

This gala . . .

Tacey's heart ached and she fought back the tears that wanted to swell up into her eyes. She desperately wanted to leave, but she also wanted to stay. She had always avoided things that had to do with *That Day*.

That Day—when her world had ended. If she was honest, That Day was like a premature *The End* to her life's book, and every day after was like a page that someone had pasted in afterwards.

Some days, were harder to live through than others.

Something in her had turned off.

After That Day; she had learned to coast through life under the radar while avoiding being underfoot.

Her life had lost its personal value—she only felt useful if others valued her.

The Woman who had taken her in after the incident had always told her exactly how expensive her life was, which had made her want to be as small as she could be; if it had been up to her, her life would not have been longer than a short appendix after those first few pages that were so full of color and life. Her life had been blanched and everything there after written with ashen grey since *that* day.

But now she had stepped out of her own book and into Edwina's storybook. She felt like a pauper stepping into the life of a princess, with glitter, glamor, and all gold that belonged to fairytales: family, fortune, and fame. She was an impostor in Cinderella's shoes and borrowed golden ball gown.

Her eyes took in the glimmering chandeliers, the tuning orchestra, the hallway of auction items . . . and then the hallway of remembrance. She looked away; that, especially, she did not want to see.

Mechanically, she listened to Mrs. Troubador's instructions and nodded accordingly. Then Mr. Troubador appeared from a back room, adjusting his bowtie.

"My little girl!" he exclaimed as he came in for a hug.

"Dad!" she said with a fake smile, as a second, quivering dart of betrayal pierced her heart.

First she had called Mrs. Troubador,"Mom," and now her husband,"Dad".

Her heart felt as if was on fire, emotions crept up her throat. She hugged him and pasted her fake smile on more firmly as way to keep back the tears. *I just want to leave.*

"How are you? Your mother said that you took a nasty fall last night."

"Much better; Miles made sure I was okay." *This is killing me; I can't play this part much longer. But I need to I need this job. It's just a job Tacey—Edwina. Keep up a brave face just a little while longer.*

Mr. Troubador turned to Miles."Thank you for taking care of my little girl."

"Glad I could, Henry."

The man smiled and turned to his wife with a kiss her."Everything almost ready, darling?"

"The last detail was the children and they are here now, so everything is set."

"Wonderful!"

Edwina looked at the little grouping that she was pretending to belong to.

Can't Edwina see how nice she has it?

The list of people Edwina had given her had seemed like paper dolls cut outs so that a child could play with them in a little cardboard house. While to her, they were not playthings but rather souls that looked at her, the fake Edwina, with a love, a joy, and a pride that Tacey couldn't—

I would give anything for a life like this. How could Edwina give this up!? The way her father looks at me—like he'd give me anything to make me happy; the love in her stepmother's eyes if she could only see it! And her brother . . . !

Her heart pounded and skipped a beat at the same time.

I've always dreamed of having a brother like him. There is definitely nothing in Tahiti that would make missing this Christmas worth it.

The first guest arrived and Tacey pulled up Edwina's notes about the gala on her phone.

Just act normal. Ask how things have been if you need to make small talk, and if they ask about school, just say you've been busy.

Act normal? How does one act normal when one is wearing a dress that would pay for all you school supplies, clothes, and lunches?

Once welcoming everyone was over and she had shown her brave face to every soul that entered. Tacey retrieved a snack and retired into the background, hovering at the edge of the crowd and hiding in shadows wherever possible

She finally slipped into"Auction Hallway," where items were on display with a short explanation of what cause it would support.

There is support for people like me? There are scholarships? There are things available—why didn't anyone tell me that there were people out there who care? Her heart ached as she walked past photographs showing what survivors of 9/11 and military families were doing together. There was laughter, joy, even color in their lives. Tacey felt robbed and betrayed: she was not the only one out there who had suffered—there were others; but they had found each other, and they had bonded, and their lives were supported and watched over with care and love; whereas she had fallen down a dark crack, and no one even knew she was there.

Memories flashed through her like lightning.

The social worker taking her to the dingy little apartment and telling her that she would have to stay there for the night until they knew what had happened to her parents.

The TV screen showing replay after replay of the plane destroying her Mommy's work building on purpose; and the question running through her mind: *Did Daddy save her?* She had told herself over and over again that they had found each other and that they were just at the hospital to make sure Mommy was okay and that they would pick her up tomorrow morning.

But they never came.

Panic was pulsing in her veins. She needed to get away; she needed to not be near people! *I don't want a fake family—I just want my own! I can't do this. I can't breathe! I need to get out of here! . . . I just want to go home!*

The auction hall was starting to fill with those looking to bid on the items.

She darted into the hall of remembrance.

Full-length photographs of people from That Day.

Moments of horror frozen in time . . . but at least no one else was there, so she could walk and clear her mind.

Just don't look at the photographs and you'll be fine.

Then, out of the corner of her eye, she saw it.

Her heart stopped beating.

That face.

She knew that face, the face of the firefighter glancing over his shoulder. Then she saw the back of his jacket—his name.

Canty.

"Daddy."

The word escaped her lips.

Tears obscured her vision.

She wanted to step forward and wrap her arms around the photograph.

If only I could hold onto him one last second! If only I could tell him not to go in there! If only I could tell him how much I love him; how much I miss him; how much I need him and Mommy.

CHAPTER

Fourteen

"Miles, honey, would you find Edwina? The auction is about to begin and her dad wants her to be with him when they auction off the item to honor her mother."

"Of course," he said with a nod.

Tacey had escaped his view not too long ago, but he knew she could not have gone far from the auction hall. *If she's not in the auction hall or in the main room, he reasoned, then she must be . . . but Edwina never goes—but, then again, she's not Edwina . . .*

He turned his steps towards the remembrance hall. Around the first corner he saw Tacey standing frozen—her body trembling, tears flowing like rivers down her cheeks—before the picture of a firefighter running towards the Twin Towers. The man was looking over his shoulder, his expression a mixture of urgency, fear, and courage. Mile's eyes fell to the firefighter's coat. CANTY was spelled in large square letters.

It's Tacey's dad. The file said her dad was a firefighter. There is no way on God's green earth that she is going to be fine getting up there and auctioning off something in honor of Edwina's mom.

"Edwina?" He said her false name softly.

She started and turned to him, her large eyes swimming in tears. He stepped closer and held out his arms. She stumbled into them, a whimper escaping her lips.

"Let's take you home," he whispered.

She nodded. putting one arm around her waist, he guided her towards the least crowded exit, digging in his pocket for his phone.

Found Edwina, but she's feeling sick, I am guessing it's all of the lights and her concussion—taking her home. Sorry, Mom.

Oh no! Is there anything I can do? His mom buzzed back.

I think there are too many people and too much stimulation after the concussion.

I'm just going to blame everything on that.

Just a really bad headache, maybe migraine. Give our apologies to the guests and don't worry. We will see you at home.

They are going to have to learn the truth after tonight. I don't know how she can maintain this role.

Their car pulled around front and he tucked her into the back, sliding in beside her. She turned away from him and leaned against the car window, trying to stifle her tears.

"I am sorry . . . I don't know what . . . I am . . ."

"It is okay, Edwina. I know you never go in there. It was brave of you," he comforted awkwardly."I'm sure that, with your concussion and all the people, you're just overstimulated."

She nodded briefly, pulling her jacket more tightly around her. They drove home in silence, save for Tacey's occasional sniffle. Once home, he opened the door and offered Tacey his hand. She took it and he helped inside, she went up the stairs and into her room closing the door gently behind her.

His phone buzzed in his pocket: it was another text from his mom.

Got a message from Grandma's butler: she fell and has asked us all to come at once. We are leaving for the airport now; meet us there as soon as you can.

He winced. Edwina and her passport were in Tahiti, while Tacey as far as he had seen in file may have never had any reason to leave the country.

How am I going to break this to Mom and Henry right now?"Hi Mom! News flash! Edwina deceived us all and is actually in Tahiti right now! There is a random girl pretending to be her." What happens if I give Tacey a chance to make a clean confession of it, and how do I get Edwina back home and to Grandma in England.

He walked up the stairs and knocked on Edwina's door.

"Who is it?" asked a broken voice from within.

"It's me, Miles."

He heard her walk towards the door, but did not open it.

"Mom just texted me. Grandma fell—we need to fly to London immediately."

The door flew open and Tacey stood before him in Edwina's pajamas and with blanket draped around her shoulders."What? Is she okay?" The concern in her face was genuine.

"She wants to see us all immediately, so—" he took a deep breath and said the fateful words, wondering how they would affect her,"—get dressed, grab your passport, and let's hit the airport."

"Wha-a-a-t?" she stammered.

"Mom and Henry are meeting us at the airport, so let's go."

"There are flights this late to London? Won't the tickets be really expensive?"

Miles shrugged slightly."You know we'll be taking *your* dad's private jet."

A blush rose in her cheeks.

"Oh! Of course we are! Umm . . ." She turned around and looked at the room, then walked to a drawer, opened it, and stared into it.

"I'll be back in a minute; I am going to get changed." Called out Miles. *Let's see what you can come up with in the five minutes I give you.*

Tacey gazed into the drawer and listened to Miles' retreating steps, knowing she'd never find a passport in there. Edwina's passport was safely in Tahiti with her, and she had no passport to try and pass off as Edwina's. She sat down on the floor of Edwina's room, biting her lower lip. *How am I going to do this? Why couldn't she have gone someplace like Florida? At least then she'd be in the same country and time zone. Can I just tell them? It would be right thing to do . . . Do I run away? Oh God, what did I get myself into simply for the love of money? My greedy soul would so love to be sitting safely on Bethany's couch right now!* Picking up the phone she texted Edwina.

Family emergency just came up! You need to come home, Your Grandma fell, and you need to go to London ASAP!!!

There was no response.

I have to call her.

She pressed the call button.

It went straight to voicemail.

What about the hotel?

Searching the phone, she found the number listed in Edwina's contacts.

It rang once before someone answered.

"Hi! I need to speak to Edwina Troubadour at once: it's a family emergency. Do you know if she is in? I tried her cell phone, but she's not answering."

"I will forward your call to her room."

There was the sound of buttons being pressed, then another ring . . . .and ring and ring and ring and ring and ring. Then it stopped and there was the sound of voices, then a violent thud as someone hung up the phone.

Her phone buzzed a moment later.

Take care of it. That is what I am paying you for! I don't want to deal with family theatrics. I'm sure it's not as bad as Grandmother says it is—she can be so dramatic.

Tacey stared at the words on the screen in shock. There was a knock at the door and she turned to see Miles standing in the doorway, leaning on the doorframe.

"Can't find your passport?"

"Ummm, no—I am not sure where I put it."

"Really?" he asked quietly."Are you sure you didn't leave it in *Tahiti?*"

Her heart flopped in her chest and her eyes widened in horror. The phone dropped to the floor.

"You're not really Edwina, are you?"

Tacey buried her face in her hands.

Closing the door behind him, Miles moved to sit on Edwina's bed.

"So, Tacey how did you get into this?"

"How did you know? How long have you known?" Her mind raced through the past twenty-four hours, wondering what exactly had betrayed her; she knew she had been playing the part miserably, but there did not seem to be one moment in particular that stood out worse than the others, where his eyes may have unveiled her disguise.

"I found out in that first hour."

"No! Why didn't you tell on me?"

"I got interested in seeing how this would all unfold, so I just thought I would wait. Besides, you made it nice around here."

"And how do you know she's in Tahiti?"

"I have a friend in intelligence who did me a favor."

"Are you angry with me?"

"Do I seem angry?"

"No . . ." She glanced up at him. He had been nothing but kind and considerate, and she realized that he must have been going out of his way to make sure that she was comfortable and that her back was covered.

"Then I am not angry. I am more amused than anything. Have you told Edwina about Grandmother yet?"

"I tried calling and texting; I even called the hotel and had them call her room. They finally answered and, uh, hung up. I did get a text back, though. Are you going to tell Mom . . . um . . . Mrs. Henderson?"

A smile flickered on his lips."What did Edwina say, exactly?"

Blushing for Edwina, she handed him the phone.

"Hmmm. Well, since she's not coming, why don't you come to London with us?"

"I don't have a passport."

His mouth twitched."I think we can fix that."

"Really?"

He nodded."If Edwina wants you to fill her shoes, I think it can be arranged. I'll take you to the passport center first thing tomorrow and get you a passport, in your own name, and you can go to London in her stead."

"But aren't passports expensive and take weeks to process?"

"We can get them in 24 hours for emergencies and family trouble like this. I'll tell Mom that you left yours at school and that we'll run and get it tomorrow, and fly over to England in a day or two."

"London? But plane tickets are so expensive! Wouldn't it be better for me to just confess?"

"Henry has several private planes. and he won't delay long enough for you to get your passport. So, I'll stay back with you and get your passport straightened out, and maybe give you some Edwina pointers."

She bit her lip and looked up at him."Have I been a terrible Edwina?"

He smiled."No, you're a wonderful Edwina: Edwina is a terrible Edwina."

She giggled and shook her head, but then a feeling of remorse swept through her."But that means I'm failing Edwina . . ."

"That's more Edwina's problem than yours. I saw the files: she didn't give you much to work with. I will admit that I did think about reporting Edwina's passport as stolen and letting her figure out how to get through customs and back to America on her own . . . but that seemed a bit much, and I didn't think Henry would be pleased."

"That would be terrible!"

Miles laughed."I'll have to be satisfied with the thought of it, then. Get some sleep. I'll fix everything."

"Are you sure? I really should just confess to everyone and admit failure. I've been so greedy . . . But I just wanted a job."

"Hey." He cut her off and moved to the floor beside her."Edwina made her choice, and you signed the contract saying you'd try. I have your back. You're going to get through this, and you're going to get every penny that Edwina owes you. Besides, I think you've been doing fine; I don't think anyone else has noticed anything amiss."

"Really?"

"Really. I think you should keep having a go at it."

Nodding, she glanced up at him. Her soul felt transparent under his gaze."Can I ask you a question?"

"Sure," Miles answered, scooting back to lean against the bed.

"Why do you call Mr. Troubadour, Henry?"

"You mean, why do I call *your dad,* Henry?" he asked with a smile.

"Yeah."

"Hmm." Miles leaned his head against the bed."You see—well, I think you've figured it out, but he's not my dad."

"Yeah. You aren't terribly warm around each other, but . . ."

"She didn't tell you much about me did she?"

"No, just that you were Miles and I should not talk to you. At all. In all caps."

"Sounds like Edwina. Anyway, my dad died in uniform. He was one of the first casualties in Iraq."

"I am so sorry." The emotions that his words triggered in her heart ran deeply: his father died fighting the thing, the ideology that caused the death of her parents. The tears started to flow for her again

"What about you? Anyone missing you while you pretend to be my sister?"

"I don't have a family anymore. I have friends, but . . . not family."

"9/11?"

"Yeah. It was my mom's first week at her new job. She was high up—and my dad was a first responder." Tears again filled her eyes.

"How old were you?"

"Three."

"You were so little."

"Yeah, a social worker came to pick me up from day-care and I was put into the foster system. My parents never even had a funeral. I lived with the same lady until I was eighteen, and then she kicked me out at midnight on my birthday, a few weeks ago."

"Grinch!"

"I was the first of 'her kids' to age out, so I didn't know it was coming."

"So, what have you been doing since?"

"I have a friend who was in the foster home with me, but she got taken out and adopted a few years ago, she's a year older than me. Thankfully, we went to the same school until she graduated. When I called her at 12:30, she came and got me and took me to her place, and I've been sleeping on her couch ever since. I've been trying to get a job, but I wasn't getting anywhere. Then my friend, her name is Bethany came across Edwina's ad a few days ago, and I think you know the rest from there."

Miles nodded slowly."Well, I think we need to get you a passport."

"Thank you, Miles."

"You're welcome. I'll go get everything straightened out with the folks, and then let's get all of your stuff together so we can get you that passport. Do you have a birth certificate?"

"Yeah, I do."

"Second form of I.D.?"

"Social security card? And my State I.D., too."

"Those sound good. Do you have them with you?"

"I left them all at Bethany's house. I thought the less of me . . ."

"Of course. We'll have to go to Bethany's, then."

"I can see if she is off and can meet us with the documents."

"That'd be great!"

"Are you really sure about this?"

Miles nodded,"Yes, I am sure about this. I'm curious to see what will happen. Besides: you did give your word to Edwina, and until she decides to fill her own shoes I think it's worth a try. Now, take those contacts out and get some sleep. We'll start first thing in the morning." He rose to his feet and offered her his hand. She took it. His strong hand grasped hers and pulled her to her feet, tugging her close. Her eyes met his; their gazes locked.

"You're going to be okay," he whispered."Goodnight."

"Goodnight."

It felt like it was the first goodnight someone had wished her—and meant it—in so, so, so long.

The door closed behind him.

Tears slipped down her cheeks as she went to the bathroom and removed the contacts. Her blue eyes stared back at her in the mirror. She missed the color of her hair, hidden under the dark brown dye. Walking back to her room, she found her old phone.

I should text Bethany—I didn't get around to doing that today.

257 missed messages, 50 missed calls.

Her battery was almost dead.

Oh no! Bethany!

Plugging her phone in, she pressed the speed dial Bethany.

Half a ring.

"Tacey!" Bethany's voice was desperate on the other side of the phone.

"Hi Bethany!"

"Are you okay? WHERE ARE YOU?"

"I'm fine! I—I got a job."

"You're really okay?"

"Yeah, there's nothing shady about this job . . . for the most part."

"No murderers? No druggies? No fiends?"

"I am safe, Bethany."

"I was so scared! I tried to call you in as a missing person, but the police said I had to wait a few more hours."

"I am so sorry, Bethany."

"No, as long as you're okay!"

"I am, but I have a question. Do you have class tomorrow?"

"Yes. I have my last final and then I am off for Christmas! You sure you don't want to come?"

"This job is going to keep me busy until after Christmas."

"Okay. Well, you have your key if you need it."

"Always."

"All right. Well, if I am going to crush this final, I've got to get back to studying; then after the test I've got a shift to make, and then: home."

"Sounds good."

"Talk to you later?"

"Talk to you later."

"Bye."

"Bye."

An insistent buzzing woke her. Rolling over, she picked up the phone Edwina had given her from where it was charging.

The caller ID said Miles was calling.

Tacey glanced at the red numbers of Edwina's clock: 4:30 a.m.

"Hello?" she answered groggily.

"Hey, sorry to wake you, but if we want to get this all done, we've got to get going. Everything is straightened out with the folks and they are on their way to England. I made an appointment at the passport center. Is your friend able to meet us?"

"No, she has a final this morning."

"Who has a final three days before Christmas?"

"She does—the professor is a little ridiculous—and then she has a shift afterwards."

"Does your place have parking?"

"No, I'm sorry, it doesn't."

"No worries; we'll drive my car in, figure out where to park, and then get everything solved from there."

"Drive into the city? Is that a good idea?"

"We will see if it is. But it's also early, so we should be able to beat the madhouse. There is always traffic in New York. I've already got parking near the passport office reserved."

"You can do that?"

"You certainly can. I know it is early, but do think you're up for going soon?"

"Of course! I'll be there in a few minutes: I just need to get dressed and grab my things and I'll be ready."

"Great! See you downstairs! And don't bother putting your contacts in, 'cause you need your real eye color for the photo, anyway."

"Thanks," she answered.

She rolled out of bed and picked a casual outfit from the closet. Everything Edwina had laid aside for her to wear seemed to be either form-fitting or paired with heels. Mixing outfits for maximum comfort, she pulled her hair back into a ponytail and grabbed the purse Edwina had given her, checking to make sure both phones and the wallet were in it, she went downstairs. Once again, Miles was waiting at the bottom of the steps.

"You weren't kidding when you said a few minutes!"

"I used to be able to get up, get dressed for school, and be out the door in five minutes."

"Impressive! Even in high school?"

"Yup!" she said with a nod.

"Didn't roll out of bed two hours early to primp and preen in front of the mirror so you'd impress the boys?"

Tacey laughed and shook her head."There was no one to impress."

Miles made a dissatisfied face."Wanna catch breakfast along the way?"

"Um, sure! As long as it is not inconvenient."

"Not at all," he said, twirling a set of keys."Today we're going to take my jeep."

"You have your own car?"

He nodded as they headed out the door, shrugging on winter coats and donning hats and gloves as they went.

There was a red jeep sitting in the garage next to the shiny town car and a small black limousine. It looked misplaced next to the two polished luxury cars.

Tacey ran around to the passenger side of the car and waited for him to unlock the doors. When the small lock button popped up, she pulled the door open and slid onto the cool leather seat.

"I should have thought to warm her up first. I'm sorry."

"I'm good."

He glanced at her and started the car, tapping the radio on.

It started belting out Christmas tunes.

"You okay with Christmas music this early in the morning?" he asked.

"Yeah!"

"Great!" He pulled out of the garage, down the driveway, and out onto the road.

Tacey smiled. *This is more like it. I like riding in cars this way. I can actually see what's going on instead of feeling like I'm blindfolded because I'm sitting in the back.*

They whizzed through the dark streets towards New York City.

They stopped at McBurgers to grab breakfast. Miles ordered egg sandwiches for both of them—since she couldn't decide what she wanted—with a simple latte for himself and a mint mocha for her which was a new experience.

"It's a beautiful city," she said as the skyline became distinct on the horizon, the skyscrapers looking like they had been dipped in gold from the rising sun. She held her hot mint mocha to her chest and sighed happily.

"First time you've been this far away from it?"

She shrugged with one shoulder."Since I was little, I guess. I haven't really had the opportunity to leave it until now."

"Tacey," Miles said, as he turned down the Christmas music to a mild hum,"If you could do anything with your life, what would you do?"

She looked over at him, puzzled by the question, but he had his eyes fixed on the road ahead of them. He turned on his blinker and changed lanes, then checked the mirrors, but still didn't look her way. She drew a deep breath.

What do I want to do with my life? I just want to survive. I don't want to be a burden to people. But if I could have any-thing, what would I want? I know what I want but he might think it is silly. She gnawed on her lower lip before deflecting the question back to him.

"Why? What do you want, Miles?"

"Hey!" he teased."That's not fair! I asked first."

"Well, then, what do you want for Christmas? Edwina said I was supposed to get you something, but I'll admit: I don't have a clue what to get. I never really paid attention to what boys were doing or what they enjoy. You already have a watch, so it would be silly to get you another one. You don't seem like a guy who plays video games, so that won't do. It's too late to get something customized and have it arrive in time for Christmas, so could you give me a few ideas?"

Miles laughed."Ah, Edwina! She would leave you with a pickle like that, wouldn't she?" His blue eyes met hers for a moment before returning to the road."But you still didn't answer my question."

"World peace, then, is what I want," she answered glibly.

He quirked an eyebrow and glanced at her out of the cor-ner of his eye."You don't seem like a girl that would answer that question that way. It's such a pat answer. What does *Tacey* want? *Really* want, when there is nothing else around."

She leaned back in her seat, feeling tears coming into her eyes. *I don't want to cry; not now. It would be silly to cry now.* She swallowed hard and pasted on a weak smile."It's not something you can find in stores."

He nodded.

The silence between them grew long.

"So, if you can't buy it, where do you find it?" Miles said quietly breaking their silence.

"It is not something you really *find*, either . . . I don't think. It is more like something you make."

He cast her a curious glance as he changed lanes again."So how do you make it?"

"I don't know," she answered."It must be the right thing at the right time. You know."

"I am not sure I do."

She bit the inside of her cheek."It is a person, or people I guess, but it is more than that. It is family. I guess, *that* is what I want more than anything. Places change, things change, even friends change, but family is family."

He drew a deep breath."It's a name; it's a place to belong when everything else changes; and the knowledge that, no matter how bad things get they'll always have your back?"

She nodded; Miles had finished her thought perfectly.

"Yeah," she added quietly, just a note above the Christmas music.

The GPS broke the silence between them as it told Miles which way to turn, and they remained quiet the rest of the way to the apartment that Tacey shared with Bethany.

"Look! I can't believe it. There's parking spot in the street right in front of our place."

Miles pulled into the space, and popped the car into park.

"Do you want to come up?"

"Only if you want me to. I can stay down here and wait."

She bit her lip, as she considered leaving him in the car."Why don't you come up? I don't know if it's clean, but it's better than waiting out here in the car."

He nodded as he turned the car off and slipped the keys into his pocket. Tacey led the way to the small apartment on the fifth floor and unlocked the door. She peeked in cautiously and called out,"Bethany?" before she entered and swung the door open for Miles.

"Sorry it's not cleaner, but it works."

"No need to apologize. So, you were staying here?"

"Yeah, I was sleeping on the couch," she said, motioning to it as she went to the dining room table, where she found a note from Bethany with a small pile of papers waiting for her.

There was the letter with her I.D. and small file with important papers title *Tacey* above it.

"She has everything here for me already."

"Awesome, do you want to change into something more comfortable for you? No offense or anything, but I don't think you and Edwina share the same style."

Tacey laughed,"No, we do not. Are you sure you don't mind?"

"Not at all. Why don't you pack a few of your things to bring back, too? I mean, you might as well be comfortable on the flight."

"You sure?"

"I don't mind a bit."

"I'll only be a few minutes," she said, stepping into Bethany's room to retrieve her clothes. She changed into her favorite pair of jeans, T-shirt, and sweatshirt, and quickly packed an overnight bag with a few of her favorite things.

"More comfortable?" Miles asked from where he sat perched on the couch.

"Yes, so much better. Thank you."

"All right—let's get rolling, then. Let me carry that," he said, offering to carry her overnight bag.

"No, it's not that heavy," she said, tightening her grip and moving it behind her back. She sidestepped around him and over to the table and scooped up her papers in her free hand.

"Okay," he said, as he stepped to open the door for her. In the few minutes they had been inside, it had decided to start snowing, and a few fragile, white flakes had started to frost the jeep. Miles opened the door for her and she tossed her overnight bag in the back seat as Miles went around the car. Starting up the car, the radio flooded the jeep with a warm, melodic baritone crooning out a classic Christmas song, backed by smooth instrumental music.

It's beginning to look a lot like Christmas . . .

Tacey smiled.

For the first time in a long time, it's actually starting to feel *like Christmas.*

CHAPTER
Seventeen

iles watched Tacey with concern. Her blue eyes were so innocent, but still so guarded. Yes, she stood on her own two feet, but she was also so afraid of stepping on others' toes. It was as if bending to other people's wills had become her nature, and it worried him. He wanted to protect her from bending too far, from finding a breaking point. Tacey needed protection, even though she didn't even realize it. But there was something more pulling him to her, like she was gravity to his spinning world; but her world was also spiraling with as much force. And yet somehow, someway, they were in the same orbit, the same revolution, looking for the same thing. Would they pull them into a black hole, or create a new galaxy of two worlds combined?

He wasn't sure yet.

He wasn't even sure if he wanted to think about it that much. But who else could he have dragged out of bed at 4:30 in the morning who wouldn't have grumbled about it at least once? Yet she had taken it in stride and followed his lead without a doubt.

She trusted him . . . but was also too elusive to lean on him for support. And, for some reason, that hurt.

He had seen her eyeing the two-dollar menu at McBurgers when she asked what he was going to order. He had noticed her biting her lip indecisively because she did not want to ask for something from him; then she had tried to pay for her half of the meal though he would not have any of it. He decided wasn't going to tell her he had paid for the passport in advance.

When she had invited him to come up to the apartment, he had jumped at the chance to see how she had been living, as well as see her in her environment and in her choice of clothes. When she had pointed out her bed which was only a couch his heart had ached.

She had gone from"not belonging" to the very fringe of existence.

He realized that Tacey was a girl on the edge of crisis. Yes, she"held it together"; yes, she had the support of a friend; but one snip of friendship, one slip into the wrong crowd, and Tacey could disappear into the dark and dangerous underworld of New York's underbelly.

Something in him wanted to hold onto her: to offer her a bridge, a shelter, an anchor, a fortress. But would she let him?

Ironic. Miles grinned to himself wryly. He had gone through most of his life trying to keep people from clinging to him, and now he had found someone who he would not mind if they did, she wouldn't. *Life is so paradoxical.*

Arriving at the 24-hour passport center, Miles parked the Jeep, carefully locked it, and together they walked into the building. The clerk took her name for the passport reservation, then ushered them to a tiny cubical where a petite Asian woman with thick, black-rimmed glasses halfway down her nose sat behind a desk.

"How can I help you?"

"I am here to get a passport," uttered Tacey almost beneath her breath.

"And for what purpose are you needing a passport?"

"Umm . . ." Tacey hesitated.

"My grandmother is in the hospital in England, and we are going together to see her" Miles answered.

"And you are?" asked the woman, eyeing him harshly.

Miles felt rather than saw Tacey's uneasy glance, it was obvious she was uncomfortable and did not want to be left alone through this process.

"Her boyfriend," he offered.

The woman's glasses shifted as she gave him a harder look, and Tacey's eyes widened. He leaned forward to whisper in her ear."I'm a boy and I'm your friend."

Her cheeks flushed as she laughed lightly.

"Now sit, sit, sit, sit! We don't have all day," said the woman.

Tacey sat down in the seat the woman was indicating, the soft blush still on her cheeks.

The process involved a lot of paperwork, and Miles watched Tacey's hands clench tighter and tighter.

She doesn't like paperwork; I wonder if being in the foster system required a lot of paperwork and office visits like this.

As Tacey passed the woman her I.D. and birth certificate, he noticed her mother's last name. *Seymour. Judith Seymour. Didn't she say her mom was a lawyer?*

Isn't one of the largest law firms in New York city Seymour and Sons? I could have sworn they were at the gala. His mouth twitched in thought and he pulled out his cell phone.

Hey Daniel. I have another favor to ask.

What's up, man?

Can you find out if a Judith Seymour married to a Tom Canty has any living family, and if she is connected to the Seymour and Sons law firm here in New York?

That is very specific.

I know.

I'm guessing this is more about your mystery woman. You know I am doing this purely for the gossip factor. It is making life more interesting over here.

Merry Christmas! Consider this my gift to you.

A minute later his phone buzzed again, but this time, Daniel was sending a picture of Edwina sitting on a beach with her friends, drinking a fruit smoothie with a wedge of pineapple, under the caption"#thereallife".

Nothing real about that stepsister of mine! You are out there having fun and having a fake"you" deal with real life.

The day progressed slowly, and while they waited for paperwork to go through, Miles and Tacey took their lunch at the hotdog stand just outside the building amid swirling snowflakes.

"I am sorry you have to go through all of this trouble for me," said Tacey,

"Not, a problem, I talked you into it; remember?"

She smiled faintly.

"Is doing all of this paperwork hard on you?" asked Miles.

She shrugged."I don't know. I just never liked when the social worker brought paperwork."

"Did you have to do a lot of paperwork?"

"More than the other kids."

"Really?"

"Yeah, but I don't know why. But the social worker was always brining paper work for me, never for the other kids. It was never comfortable; I was so much trouble with all of that extra work."

"Really? . . . I noticed that your mom's name is different than your dad's."

"Yeah, I guess she kept it after they got married. I think it was because she got her lawyer license under that name and didn't want to go through all the paperwork to change it, or something. I remember them talking about it once."

"Did you have family?"

She tilted her head quesioningly.

"Like, aunts and uncles,"

"No, it was just Mom and Dad."

"Of course, because no one took you in. because how could anyone pass up a treasure like you."

"That's not true, But why?"

"I was just wondering if you'd ever heard of the big law firm *Seymour and Sons*."

Tacey looked at him blankly and shook her head, but a question blossomed in her eyes as she took another bite of her hotdog.

"I suppose we should go back in and get this thing finished." sighed Miles when Tacey had finished her hot dog.

"Yeah, we don't want to make her wait. And what if I have my passport ready?"

There was a tone of delight in her voice.

It was a long afternoon but at last, Tacey had her passport, and they could walk out of the doors. Tacey clutched the small blue booklet with the gold embossing on the front in her hands as they walked back to the jeep."I didn't think I would ever own one of these. I thought only people in movies and rich folks had them."

"Not quite."

She turned to him with bright eyes."You know, I always wanted to go to England, ever since I was girl. We read Mark Twain's *The Prince and the Pauper* in grade school and it was my favorite! And, sometimes, because I had the same last name as Tom Canty, I would pretend that I had been a princess switched at birth and . . . well, it's silly, really."

"Is it?"

"Silly little girl stuff; things like that don't happen in real life."

"If you say so. Come on, let's hit the airport with that new shiny passport of yours."

"But I haven't packed any of Edwina's things . . ."

"I got a text from Mom when you were finalizing things she said that she had the maid pack everything we'd need and it's waiting for us at the airport."

Eighteen

They hopped into the jeep once again and cruised out into evening New York gridlock traffic

They had been sitting in nearly the same spot for an hour. Miles turned the radio off as a female singer began yet another rendition of *It's Beginning to Look a Lot Like Christmas.* "You'd think they'd play something besides the same ten songs," he sighed as he slumped in his seat. He checked his cell phone and answered a text; nothing in traffic had changed for fifteen minutes.

"Will we be late?" asked Edwina.

"Well, it's a private jet, so I we can't be exactly late but, yeah, the poor pilot will probably have the jet fueled and ready long before we get there."

"I'm sorry."

"Why are you sorry?"

"If I wasn't here, you wouldn't be doing this."

Miles' countenance shifted."Tacey, when was the last time you told someone no?"

She tilted her head and shrugged her shoulders."Why are you asking?"

"You could have told my sister 'no' about this job, but you said yes. Honestly, the terms and conditions were rather horrific."

"It was the first job I was really offered."

"And so you took it?"

She nodded.

"Did you negotiate at all?"

"No."

There was another long pause.

"Tacey, this—this is kind of personal, but when was the last time . . . someone said . . . I love you? To you?"

Tacey grew still as a shiver ran down her spine. There was such an ache for those words in her life: It was the last thing her parents had told her.

Tacey was still.

Miles glanced at her. Tears filled her eyes and her lips were pressed together.

"Tacey?"

"Not since—since *that* day . . ." her voice quivered.

Never had Miles been more grateful for a gridlock of cars! He shifted the car into park and reached for her over the console. She turned to him, burying her face in his shoulder and curling into a fetal position on the seat of the jeep. Tears, silent and deep, soaked his shirt.

"Tacey, I am so sorry. I am so, so sorry."

"It's okay," came, muffled, from out from his shirt.

"No, it isn't," he whispered. "You should have been protected and loved and cherished; you shouldn't have to be alone."

Car horns honked behind them. He glanced at traffic and realized he needed to move. Tacey pulled away from him, another "I'm sorry" dropping from her lips.

"Don't be," he said, shifting the car into gear and taking her hand, her head slowly coming to rest on his shoulder.

They drove in silence the rest of the way to the airport, too many words wanting to be said to break out a single one.

Twenty

Jacey sat in the posh leather plane seat, her heart racing as images from That Day flashed through her mind. Planes, buildings, ash filling the sky—being alone, and then the starkness of life without love.

Miles sat in the seat next to her, comparatively relaxed, pressing on keys to spell out a text.

"Are you sure we'll get there?"

"Hmm? Yeah, the snow is dwindling, and we'll be just fine once we're flying."

She took a deep breath and gazed fixedly out the window.

His hand brushed hers and she jumped pulling away.

"Are you scared?"

"I've never been in a plane before, and all I can think of is—is the Towers."

"I am sitting here, right beside you, and I am telling you, we are going to be just fine. This pilot has flown for Henry for years. He's going to fly us straight to London; nothing bad is going to happen."

"Promise?"

"Promise."

Her hand reached for his and he took it tightly, slipping his fingers between hers. She looked up into his blue eyes, and strangely, she felt at home. Things were going to be all right.

"Why don't you try to get some rest? We will arrive in London early in the morning, and most likely the chauffer will take us directly to see Grandmother. I'd suggest that you get some sleep before then; it's been a long day."

"Aren't you going to give me 'Edwina pointers'?"

"After you get some rest."

"After the plane takes off, maybe?"

"Sure."

Twenty-One

Tacey clung to his hand until after takeoff, then slowly drifted to sleep, her head coming to rest on his shoulder.

He pulled out his phone and connected to the inflight Wi-Fi. He had some research he was dying to dig into. Typing in"Judith Seymour," he came across some old articles.

Judith Seymour leaves family firm for love

Judith Seymour named New York's most successful Woman Lawyer

Judith Seymour returns to family firm after reconciliation

The last article she was in was when her name appeared on the casualty list of 9/11. He looked up her picture and realized that Tacey looked very much like her mother.

An email came from Daniel and he opened it.

Hey! Turns out you were right! Tacey Canty is actually an heiress!

Miles glanced down at the sleeping Tacey beside him.

How do you not know that? How was all this hidden from you? You weren't so far from the truth after all, you were told you were a pauper when you were the little princess.

He gently shifted Tacey to lean against the window, and left his seat to go to a small back room that served as an office. Pulling up the laptop that was there.

The Charity Gala information has to be somewhere in here; I just need to find the Seymours' contact information so I can give them a call.

After some serious searching, he found what he was looking for and made an internet call.

"Hey! This is Miles Henderson, we spoke at my mom's Charity Gala. This is a huge jump but I happen to know a Tacey Canty—daughter of a Jane Seymour. I am wondering if there is a chance that you're looking for her. Anyway, give me a call at" (he gave him his number) "if you have questions. I'll be in London soon, so I might be harder to get a hold of, thanks, bye."

He hung up the phone with the hope that he had done the right thing. Something just did not sit right: if the family had reconciled, then Tacey should have been raised by her uncle, right?

He leaned back in the office chair and thought deeply. *I really should go give her some Edwina pointers, but I don't want her to be Edwina! But if she's to pull the wool over Grandmother's eyes—as well as everyone else's—I'll have to tell her a few things. But how do you tell someone who has never said no to anyone in their life to be abrupt and abrasive? Does Tacey even have what it takes to fill Edwina's shoes? She has the looks, perhaps, but definitely not attitude and personality.* Getting up, he returned to the main cabin, where Tacey still slept.

His phone alerted him that it was dying. Finding the cord, he plugged it into charge and sat down. Leaning back, he took a short nap. When he woke, it would be battle stations.

CHAPTER
Twenty-Two

The grey outside of the window gave way to a glimpse of skyline and black tarmac as the plane landed with a bounce that made her gasp.

"Are you okay?" came a groggy voice beside her.

"Oh, I didn't mean to wake you!"

He had been rather cute fast asleep, a gentle snore escaping him from time to time. Tacey blushed at her thought, as it raced back to what he had said the day before about being her boy friend—friend that is a boy, that is. No one in her life had expressed that much interest in her . . . and it wasn't just interest. It was *care;* she felt safe, she felt—something. She transferred her gaze back to the semi-foggy tarmac.

"So, this is England?"

"It is," said Miles, with a stretch and sigh. "So, what do you say we get coffee once we are through immigration?"

"We are in England. Aren't we supposed to drink tea?" she teased.

His smile was brief. "This American boy drinks coffee; we dumped that other stuff in the harbor years ago."

Tacey giggled.

"But my lady shall get tea if she pleases," he said, putting on a fake British accent.

Tacey laughed and replied, in her best imitation, "I think I'd like that, good sir."

"Excellent."

Once through immigration, Miles stopped at the first international coffee chain shop he found and ordered a cup of black coffee for himself and a London Fog for Tacey.

"It seems a pity to be drinking tea out of paper cups, doesn't it? I feel like is should be more regal."

"Now that sounds like something Edwina would say!" said Miles with a smile.

"Does it?"

He nodded.

"What else would Edwina do?"

There almost seemed to be pain in his eyes as he looked at her.

"There would be more firmness in her step, and fewer apologies for one."

"What else?"

He squinted at her."Let's try just those two for now."

"Okay," she said, with a small skip.

"And no skipping," Miles added.

She turned around and made a face at him."Edwina's no fun."

"You're telling me!"

As Miles had predicted, the chauffeur was waiting for them."Your grandmother would like me to bring you both around to the hospital first thing."

"Of course, but we will need to change and freshen up before we see her," Miles said.

She saw Miles eyeing her outfit. Somehow they had both forgotten to have her change before they landed. Her clothes were certainly something that Edwina would not be caught dead wearing.

"Of course," said the chauffeur.

They slid into the backseat of the town car and Tacey had to remind herself not to press her nose against the glass as she stared at things that, before this, had seemed to exist only in books and movies.

They pulled up before a hospital entrance and got out of the car. Tacey quickly selected an outfit from the carefully packed garment bag along with a pair of glamorous flats that were a better choice than her New-York-City-friendly sneakers. Upon entering the hospital, Tacey slipped into the nearest restroom and changed, patting on some makeup to make the transformation complete.

With her New York City street clothes tucked under one arm, she reappeared before Miles and did a full circle.

"How do I look?"

"Good."

"Good! Now to put these clothes back in the car before we visit Grandmother!"

Tacey quickly tucked the clothes in her own overnight bag in the trunk of the car and rejoined Miles.

"Are you ready?"

Tacey took a deep breath."Ready as I'll ever be, though I should have reviewed the information card that Edwina gave me for Grandmother before doing this! I was just so . . . taken away by everything! England is beautiful!"

"Isn't it? Now, remember, be brisk."

"I will."

They arrived at the room that the nurse had said was Margaret Troubadour's room.

Miles led the way,"Grandmother! How are you?"

"I am fine; how are you and *Edwina*?"

"We are doing well," said Miles. snatching up the spokesperson role to sell Tacey as Edwina.

Tacey smiled and nodded.

The white-haired woman laughed a little, and then louder.

"What's so funny, Grandmother?" Miles asked.

"Oh, I don't know. Now, the two of you come here and sit down for a minute."

Obediently, they sat.

She stared at Tacey for a while, and then at Miles. Finally, the elderly woman settled back against her pillows with a satisfied chuckle.

"Miles, *that* is not Edwina."

"Grandmother . . . !" protested Miles.

"Don't 'grandmother' me like that! I know a thing when I see it, and you've never looked at Edwina that way."

"Grandmother!" Miles protested.

"And, Edwina has never walked that way."

"Grandmother, it is really me—your Edwina! I've just really worked really hard this semester. I'm glad to be with family with Christmas, though; it's wonderful to have a break from all that studying!"

"Let me tell you, young lady: you might be pulling the wool over all of their eyes, but you aren't pulling it over mine! I see the way Miles looks at you, and I know he never looked at his stepsister that way! Besides, my granddaughter would have been huffing about how intolerable this hospital room is. No, you aren't my granddaughter. So, who are you, really?"

"First Miles, and now you," sighed Tacey, covering her face with her hands.

The elderly lady laughed again and Tacey looked up."I'm actually a step ahead of you," Grandmother said."I have been, all the time. I've been secretly paying one of Edwina's friends to spy on her, since this old lady has to do *something* for amusement. Edwina is in Tahiti, and you're trying to pretend to be her; what kept you from getting here sooner was your passport, but Miles got that all fixed for you, I see," she said, pulling out a manilla file folder and opening it. There were 8x10 photographs of Tacey and Miles outside of the passport office eating hotdogs, pictures of them at the apartment when they got Tacey's clothes, and pictures of them walking to the car. Also in the folder were snapshots of Edwina in Tahiti.

"Grandmother! You've been spying on us?" Miles said reproachfully.

"I spy on everyone. No one writes, texts, or calls. How else am I supposed to know what you are all up to? Besides, I am an old lady with too much time and too much money."

Tacey glanced at Miles in despair, and he shrugged in reply shaking his head in disbelief.

Edwina's summary of her grandmother ran through her mind: *Grandmother is the sharp Matriarch of the family, and her word is law. Don't do anything stupid or rash! You'll always end up doing whatever Grandmother wants, no matter what. Don't get too close to her: she, if anyone, will notice the swap.*

Well, she knew all right.

"I'm surprised that you didn't report her passport as stolen," Grandmother said, winking at Miles.

"I was tempted to."

"Good boy. I applaud your self-control, as I am appalled at Edwina's insensitivity. Is she on her way over?"

"No," answered Tacey meekly.

"Does she know I am bound up in the hospital like a turkey trussed for Christmas dinner?"

"I sent her a message and tried to call her."

"You should show that text to Grandmother, *Edwina*."

"Call her Tacey; I rather like that name. And what is it with a message from my granddaughter?"

"I am not sure if it's really a good idea . . ." Tacey hesitated.

"Are you afraid I'll cut her out of the will or something?"

"I—I don't know," stuttered Tacey.

"Show it to me; I'm hatching a plan." Her blue eyes twinkling with ideas.

Tacey glanced at Miles and he nodded.

Unlocking the phone, she pulled up the text from Edwina and showed it to Grandmother.

"Oh! Is this her opinion of me? Indeed! Well, what if we give her a taste of her own medicine? What is she paying you?"

Tacey named the amount.

"I'll double it, if you'll help me with the next part."

"What?"

"You see, people never appreciate a person until they are gone. Now, how good are you at crying?"

"Crying?" Tacey asked.

"Yes, crocodile tears; great *big* ones."

"Okay, I suppose . . ."

"Very good. You see, I want you to go back to my lovely townhouse and announce that I am dead. Text Edwina, too; I want her in London A.S.A.P."

"What?" asked Tacey puzzled.

The old woman laughed."You see, two can play this game, and I think the perfect gift for Edwina this Christmas is a good surprise. Miles, tell Robinson to put plan '*Ashes*' into motion."

"Grandmother . . ." said Miles with a long-drawn-out tone.

"When you are as old as I, you can have only so much fun, and I intend to have all I can. I've always wanted to go to my own funeral and this is a grand way to do it, without the bother of actually having to die. Just be sure you cry great big tears for me, because I don't think anyone else is going to."

"I'll try my best," said Tacey.

"Excellent! Miles, I want you to go home and announce my death, and then take this darling girl out for grand shopping spree at Harrods. I'm sure neither of you brought clothes fit for a funeral. While you're at it, get me a box of caramel chocolates; they don't serve such food here. Thankfully, I won't be here much longer, so I'll send you the address where you should come visit me and bring me my chocolates."

"Grandmother," said Miles, with a twinkle in his eye,"Did you really fall, or did Robinson begin plan *'Fall'* for you?"

"You should never question your elders, young man, or ask such important questions."

"You and Edwina were cut from the same cloth."

"Don't I know it. The problem is, as an old lady, I have little to occupy me but my schemes, and this *Project Fall* seemed like a particularly good one. Besides, I really am getting too old to be crammed into a metal can to cross the Atlantic, private jet or otherwise."

"Did you do all of this just get Edwina's attention?"

Grandmother gave Miles a pointed look."I told you to go directly home and then to Harrods. I'll have Robinson text you further instructions. No one will notice you two slip off;

they will have to go see the lawyer and the undertaker right away, anyway."

They rose and Tacey gratefully took the arm Miles offered her as they walked out the door.

"That was kind of . . ." trailed Tacey.

"Shocking?"

"Yeah, shocking."

"I wonder how Edwina will take the news?"

"I should text her, shouldn't I?"

"I would think so."

"I think I'll wait until we get to the car."

The chauffeur was waiting outside to take them to Grandmother's house.

They slipped into the car, the weight of what they were about to do pressing heavily on Tacey's shoulders. Settling into her seat Tacey pulled out the phone and started typing a message to Edwina.

"She'll get it right as she gets up; that's a rude awakening, isn't it?"

"Well, a rude awakening for a rude person might be just the thing!"

Tacey shook her head doubtfully and finished her message.

Arrived in London. Your grandmother passed away this morning. Please come to London A.S.A.P.

"I feel awful sending this to her."

"You're under Grandmother's orders."

"It's not being truthful, though."

Miles held out his hand."Here, give it to me. I'll send it."

Tacey placed the phone in the palm of his hand. He took it, pressed *send*, and gave it back to her.

"There—now you didn't do it."

"But I played a part in the deception."

"You're growing a conscience *now*? After taking a job where you get paid you to deceive us?"

She pursed her lips, trying to find the words she wanted to say.

"We're getting close to Grandmother's house; you might want to get some tears up before we get there so they don't have to appear out of nowhere when we announce *The News*."

Tacey surprised herself: the tears weren't nearly as hard to come by as she had expected. The whole situation—everything she had gone through in the past few days—made her want to cry for so many reasons sad, yet happy. She glanced at Miles: she had never dreamed she'd meet someone like him—someone who would ask the questions he had asked the day before in his Jeep. It just wasn't something that she had expected.

The vehicle stopped before an elegant white townhouse. Miles moved into action before the Chauffeur even opened the door offering her his hand. They walked up the steps and Miles rang the doorbell. An elderly gentleman answered the summons.

"Good morning Mr. Miles and Miss—*Edwina*." he said, with a raised eyebrow looking at their hands clasped in a tight hold.

"Good morning, Robinson." Said Miles."I'm here to tell you to start plan '*Ashes*,' and I am to make the announcement to the family."

"Oh dear," said Robinson, a twinkle in his eye."I will start at once. The family is starting breakfast. I am sure you do not mind showing yourselves in, since you are Americans, and so independent."

"We don't mind in the least."

Tacey glanced at the house as they walked: it was magnificent, almost as if it were a set for a show. Lavish Christmas decorations were in precise, elegant order.

"It feels like a movie," she whispered to Miles.

"It's about to feel even more so in a minute. Almost like one of those dramatically cheesy Christmas specials."

Tacey choked back a laugh, and they entered the dining room. Instantly she recognized Aunt Flora and Uncle Arnold, and their three young children. Uncle Arnold having chosen to marry later in life.

"Good morning Miles, Edwina. Why, what's wrong? You look—" said Miles mother.

"Grandmother is dead," burst out Tacey, the tears coming readily enough as she said the words. She turned and buried her face in Miles' sleeve.

"What? She was in perfect health when we left her last night," said Henry Troubadour rising to his feet.

"It happened just before we got there," explained Miles."It was a heart attack or stroke—I don't remember which—and she's gone. The hospital would have called, but since we were there, they thought it best that we deliver the news."

Complete shock lingered in the room.

Arnold rose from the table."We should make arrangements; I'll contact the undertaker."

"And I'll call the lawyer. Maybe we can get everything set in order before the new year . . ." said Henry.

"Yes, that would be good," agreed Arnold.

Tacey emerged from Miles' sleeve to see tears in the men's eyes as they left the room. Their wives following after with comforting words and support.

The three small children sat in wonderment. They knew what"death" meant, but they had not experienced the emotions that went with it.

"I didn't bring anything suitable for a funeral, so I suppose we should go shopping," said Miles."Will you help me pick out a suit, Edwina?"

"Of course," she said, following him half blindly as she wiped her eyes.

Slipping back out into brisk morning London air, they skipped nimbly down the steps into the waiting car.

"Harrods, please, driver," said Miles.

"Right away; this package is for you, from Robinson."

"Thank you," said Miles, taking the small parcel from the driver's hand and opening it. Tacey peeked over his shoulder to see the contents of the envelope, which included several large pound notes and a list of things to buy.

Caramels

Cheese

Crackers

Chocolates

Biscuits

Tea

I also have some things on hold at the jewelry counter. It is paid for; simply mention my name to pick it up.

"Grandmother has quite the list!" said Miles.

"This is going to be such fun!" sighed Tacey in delight."What is Harrods like?"

"Quite interesting! I think you will enjoy it."

"You really think so?"

"Just wait and see."

They got lost in Harrods, and after over an hour, Miles' phone buzzed. He glanced at the message: it was from Grandmother.

I am waiting.

They left Harrods after picking up the small box tucked into a gift bag at the jewelry counter and checking the list three times over.

The chauffeur picked them up and drove them to a quieter side of town where there were more posh townhouses. As the car parked on the street, Miles looked up to see Grandmother at the door waiting for them.

"I think we kept her waiting too long," said Miles.

"Oh dear," mourned Tacey."But it was so fun."

The chauffeur opened the door and they slid out and walked up the small garden walkway to the front door.

"Way to keep an old lady who's been living on hospital food for two days waiting," she affectionately bristled.

"Harrods was amazing, though I'm so sorry we kept you waiting, Grandmother," said Tacey.

"Nothing like that in New York City?"

"Oh! I wouldn't really know . . . But it was marvelous!"

"I am glad to hear it; now where are those caramels? I need one post haste."

Miles obediently dug through the bags and pulled out the caramels.

"Put the spread out on the table. I've already put the kettle on. Tea will be served immediately."

"Isn't it a little early for tea?" asked Miles.

"It's never too early for a cuppa!" answered Grandmother as she disappeared back into the little kitchen.

Tacey helped him spread out the treats they had purchased while Grandmother came out with a steaming kettle.

Sitting down, they ate, talked, and drank until a third unusually large yawn escaped from Tacey.

"Tacey, you look tired out. I don't think jet lag agrees with you," said Grandmother.

"Oh, I'm fine. I slept most of the flight." Tacey tried to hide another yawn behind her hand.

"Well, why don't you take a nap, anyway? I have things to discuss with Miles."

She blinked twice.

"You've had several traumatic days, all in a row," Miles added quietly."Sleep won't hurt you."

"There is a guest room just down the hall. It's barely 8 a.m. in New York, so go and at least close your eyes for a spell."

Tacey finally surrendered and, with a sleepy nod, shuffled to the guest door and closed it behind her.

Miles turned his attention to Grandmother."There is something you want to discuss with me?"

"Your future."

"My future?"

"I haven't said anything until now, since you seemed pretty set on your own ways, but now . . ."

"Now *what*?"

"I think you have to think about other things. You've proven your point being in the military and doing your own thing. But you need a career, and what is more your family needs you. What are you going to do about it?"

"Why are you asking?"

"Miles, what are you thinking about that girl? What are your intentions?"

"Grandmother!"

"I can read the look in your eye. You never dated seriously, even in high school; you've avoided relationships and people—and now you're bending over backwards to get a passport and make all of this chaos work for this girl."

"Grandmother!"

"It's my business to meddle, since it seems your parents are too busy to notice that she is not Edwina." She shoved the small jewelry box that he had picked up at Herrod's across the table to him."Open that."

Opening it, inside he found a square-cut diamond set in simple gold band.

"Grandmother."

"Now, you know you are one of my favorite grandchildren, even though it's by marriage and not by direct bloodline. If you love that girl, the way I think you do . . ."

He slammed the lid back onto the box."Grandmother!"

"Miles, you realize that, once this Christmas is over, the chances of you seeing her again are very slim unless you move swiftly. She is a nobody, so she will most likely slip back into her part of society, where the cracks are very easy to fall through."

"I won't let her slip."

"But she may let herself slip, if she doesn't think she is worth it."

"Grandmother."

"You keep saying that."

"I know. But I think it's too soon to say anything. Besides, I've made contact with her family."

"Her family?"

He smiled. *So, Grandmother doesn't know everything.* "Her mother was a famous lawyer who gave it all up to marry the man she loved. Her family split with her, and had only recently—well, as recently as in 9/11—made up with her when she died in the 9/11 attacks. Tacey doesn't even know they exist."

Grandmother's eyes lifted in interest. "Then how do you know?"

"I don't know the whole story, but I intend to find out if they want to be a part of her life."

As if on cue, his phone rang. The information for the phone number he had called popped up on his screen.

"I need to take this, Grandmother."

"Very well; ignore me."

"It's her uncle."

"At eight am in the morning two days before Christmas?"

Miles offered her a shrug as he answered the call."Hello, this is Miles Henderson."

"Miles, about the message you left me last night: you said you know a Tacey Canty. How did you suspect that she is related to us?"

"A Judith Seymour is her mother. From the photos I saw online they look alike, and I saw her name on Tacey's birth certificate."

"Please tell me Tacey's not dead," the man said breathlessly.

"No."

"Thank the Lord—does she still hate us?"

"Hate you?" Miles asked.

There was silence on the other end of the phone.

"She doesn't even know that you exist, as far as I know."

"What do you mean?" asked Mr. Seymour.

"She told me she had no relatives."

"Do you have any photos of her?"

"I don't think—" his eye fell on the folder that Grandmother had of the two of them."Actually, yeah, sort of."

"Could you send them to this number?"

"Sure; just hold for a moment." He flipped open the manilla folder and took pictures of the photos with his phone. There was one with her smiling at him, but he cropped himself out of the picture. He put them in a text message and hit send.

"The photos are on their way to you."

"Fantastic. Stay on the line?" said the anxious voice on the other end of the phone.

"Of course."

"Ah! Here they are, oh dear me. She looks just like Judith." There was an agonized groan on the other end of the line."You say she knows nothing about us?"

"Not as far as she told me."

"Is she in college?"

"No."

"Any plans for college?"

"None; she's looking for a job."

"Even with her trust fund?"

Mile's heart twisted."She's been living at a friend's house, sleeping on the couch. I don't think she knows anything about a trust fund."

"Those thieving liars! I knew I didn't trust the social worker. Where is she now?"

"With me in London. It is a long story."

There was a long pause.

"I cannot leave at this minute, but I will fly over tonight once I conclude my business here. I *must* confirm things for myself."

"Of course."

"Thank you, Miles. I will be in touch."

The man hung up.

"What was that all about?" Grandmother asked.

"It sounds like Tacey has a concerned uncle who wants to get involved in her life."

"Well, well, well! Things *are* getting interesting. Maybe, I should die more often."

"Grandmother, if you die more than once, people will start getting suspicious."

"Oh, will they now?" She wiggled her white eyebrows playfully."I promise not to make a regular habit out of it, but it's quite fun at least this once. I got a text about Edwina! She is headed to the airport to come straight to London. They'll have to refuel along the way, but it seems that Edwina is finally on her way!"

"Apparently dying will do it. It's going to be an interesting 24 hours, to say the least."

Twenty-Three

Tacey opened her eyes. The sheets smelled of vanilla and roses, which had made for the most scrumptious sleep she had ever had. Turning, she looked up at the ceiling. There was something delightful about this house: you could feel its age and sense the history that it held in its walls, what it had witnessed. It felt like a happy sort of house, a house she wanted to stay in forever. Stretching, she turned once again to glance at the clock to her right.

2:35.

Tacey shot straight up in bed. *Oh no! I planned on taking only a short nap, not sleeping the entire day away!*

Just then, there was a knock at the door."Tacey?"

"Miles?" she answered, swinging her feet to the floor.

The door cracked open and his blond head poked in."Rest well?"

"Far better than I intended to."

A smile crossed his face."We need to get back to the other house; they'll miss us if we're gone much longer."

"Of course, how is Grandmother?"

"I am doing just fine!" called the woman, from the other room.

Tacey smiled.

"She has another round of tea ready; then we will head back to the house."

"Sounds good."

"What are we going to tell them if they ask why we were gone so long?"

"First, I doubt that they've noticed—they haven't tried to contact either of us," he said, holding up her phone."Grandmother said her lawyer is aware of the truth, of course, and is going through with the charade beautifully. The undertaker, too, has all the instructions, so nothing will *actually* happen. However, Edwina is finally on her way to the airport, so she'll be here tomorrow sometime just in time for the reading of the will."

"The tea is ready if the two are you are ready to stop gabbing," called Grandmother from the sitting room.

A soft blush crept up Miles' cheek."Yes, allow me let you at least get up before I talk your ear off." He closed the door behind him and Tacey rubbed the last bit of sleep out of her eyes. She had not realized how much she had needed that nap. Walking over to the mirror, she tugged her clothes that were wrinkled beyond repair without an iron. *Edwina would probably be furious.*

After a few brushes through her hair, she felt like she was at least semi-presentable. She joined Miles and Grandmother at the table and sat down for a cup of black tea.

Miles nudged the sugar bowl in her direction, so she took two lumps and stirred them in the bottom of her teacup, with a splash of milk.

"Good rest?" asked Grandmother.

"Too good, perhaps," she said with a sigh that was mixed with a giggle.

Grandmother smiled. "Miles and I had a good time catching up while you rested, and, like he said, Edwina is finally underway."

"What am I going to do? How do we make the exchange of Edwina's?"

Grandmother shrugged. "You only have a few more hours left to play Edwina, so I suggest you play it well."

"I'm guessing Edwina wouldn't be caught dead looking like this," Tacey said, motioning to her wrinkled outfit.

"Oh! That reminds me! I sent for a new outfit for you," said Grandmother. "You're right that Edwina wouldn't be caught dead wearing what you're wearing now, especially when she's in London. The outfit for you is hanging up in the hall closet; go take a peek."

Tacey rose from the table, walked to the small hall closet, and opened it, where she found an all-black outfit comprised of an oversized black sweater and a calf-length skirt. A shoe box with a smart pair of black oxford heels sat on the ground beneath.

"All of this?"

"All," reassured Grandmother.

"It's so lovely!"

"I figured you should have a new mourning outfit. It's still stylish, but I think it's more your style."

"Thank you, Grandmother!" she said, turning to the woman with an affectionate glance. Somehow the elderly woman was the easy to love. But, then again, Tacey knew who Grandmother *really* was. Skipping across the small room to the old woman, she leaned down and gave her a kiss on the cheek.

"Oh, you dear child, just sit and drink your tea."

Tacey sat down and sipped the perfectly sweetened cup of refreshing and fortifying liquid.

As soon as she had finished, she slipped back into the bedroom where she had napped and changed into her new outfit. She came out with a twirl to show it off. "Thank you do much Grandmother."

"You are most welcome. Now, the two of you get going back to my house and behave like mourning grandchildren, and don't give a breath of my shenanigans away."

They bade her adieu, Miles leaned down to kiss her on the cheek, then, with subdued laughter, Tacey and Miles walked out the door to the waiting town car, side by side. The car started slowly moving down the streets on what felt like, to Tacey, the wrong side of the road.

"It's so strange the way they drive over here," said Tacey

"Hmm?"

"I know I haven't been in many cars but it's so funny to watch traffic going what feels like the opposite way round."

He laughed slightly."Well, I hear it helps if you pretend that you're a knight in a jousting tournament, since you want your right hand to oppose your opponent."

"Is that why they are the way that they are?"

He shrugged."I'm not sure; that's just what I've heard."

They drove several more minutes in silence.

"Is something bothering you Miles?"

"Hmm?" he said, turning to her.

"I said, is something bothering you? You've been awfully quiet."

"Am I? It must just be that I'm tired."

"It feels like it's more than that."

"Does it?"

She nodded."Something is on your mind."

"Perhaps something is—perhaps something isn't," he said with a half-smile.

"Are you going to tell me?"

His smile grew a little larger, and then he sighed. "Maybe—sometime."

She nodded, sensing he didn't want to share with her. Pulling slightly away, she looked out the window.

"I'm not looking forward to tomorrow being your last day with us," Admitted Miles.

She turned back to face him.

"I've enjoyed your company—and everything we've done in the last few, crazy days. I don't want to say goodbye."

She bit her lip."I guess I hadn't thought of that . . . somehow. With Edwina arriving tomorrow, my contract will be up with her. How will I get back to America?"

"Don't worry about that. I know we can get that covered. Tacey . . . do you know an Edward Seymour?"

"Can't say that I do."

He nodded."Ever heard his name?"

"No, I can't say I have."

To this he only nodded.

"Why?"

"Just curious."

"Do you think I might have family somewhere?"

"It just bugs me that you don't."

She smiled softly."I had a family for this Christmas—that is what matters."

"It's not even Christmas yet."

"But it *feels* like Christmas." She reached for his hand. He took hers and squeezed.

"I want you to have so much more of a Christmas."

She smiled back at him."You still have not told me what you want for Christmas. Edwina is going to be mad if I have not thought of a Christmas gift by the time she gets here."

He looked keenly at her, then shook his head.

"What is it?"

"It's nothing."

"No, I saw it in your eyes. You know what you want."

"I can't ask for it."

"What is it?"

"Tacey, I'll tell you when I am ready, but until then—" he smiled at her, but there was pain in his eyes"—you'll just have to wait."

The look in his eyes. She could not tell him that it was giving her butterflies in the pit of her stomach . . . that she wanted to unbuckle her seat belt and slide over just to be close to him . . . that and her heart was skipping beats . . .

"Here we are," said the driver, breaking into her thoughts.

The door opened and they slid out of the car and stood on the narrow walkway leading up to the house.

"We have to be sad now." Sighed Miles.

"All I have to do is think about leaving tomorrow, and I *am* sad."

His hand squeezed hers."Come on. Let's go inside."

Twenty-Four

He had to get them both inside or he would drop to one knee on the sidewalk right then. The ring Grandmother had given him felt as if it was burning a hole in his breast pocket, like it had been screaming in his mind all afternoon.

He knew exactly what he wanted for Christmas.

Her. *Them.*

But he couldn't ask.

He had no future to offer her—not yet. The poor girl did not even know who she was yet.

She needs stability and reassurance before a man drops on one knee before her and proposes. She doesn't know she has the whole world at her fingertips, as the daughter of Judith Seymour and Tom Canty. She is an heiress We don't have all the details, and I need Edward Seymour to get here so we can talk.

They walked inside and he dropped her hand unwillingly before handing his coat to the butler, who looked highly amused.

"Dinner will be served at six sharp—if anyone has the appetite for it."

"Where is everyone?" asked Miles.

"The children are upstairs amusing themselves; or, at least, that is what I hope they are doing. The rest are down in the office with the lawyer settling affairs. The reading of the will shall happen tomorrow at one o'clock sharp."

"The will? Tomorrow? Before the funeral?"

"It is how your grandmother wishes it," returned the butler, eyeing him impassively, though his eyes twinkled.

"Of course, of course."

"Would the Miss care for a tour of the house?" The butler's attention shifted to Tacey as she gave him her coat.

"That would be very helpful," replied Tacey with a smile.

"Then allow me to lead the way."

"Aren't you coming, Miles?"

"He knows the house quite well, I am sure," said the butler, significantly.

Yes, I know the house quite well, and I know what room is mine; now to beat my retreat while I can!

Arriving at his room on the second floor, he flopped down on an old-fashioned bed that creaked familiarly under him. He smiled. Grandmother hadn't changed a thing about this room, and for some reason, he found that delightful. Her words from their talk that afternoon started running through his mind.

"Come work with me in London, Miles. You need a fresh start. You'd be a part of the company, but you wouldn't be directly under Henry's thumb . . . ." He remembered his mother's suggestion that he work with the charity foundation in New York. If he took Grandmother's offer he wouldn't be working with his mother; but somehow this job felt less like charity. The position at the company would be a bigger step towards harder things. He would be honoring his mother's wishes of getting a job with the family, but he would also be more independent than if he was working for her. A job at the company would create a future, or, at least, it would get him started. Maybe his mom's charity would be something he would move into, but he knew that he still needed to transfer into adulthood in both of their eyes. Henry saw him as a rebellious young man who had been unwilling to come under his authority, and his mother was a hovering hen anxious for his welfare. This opportunity though. *Thank you Grandmother,* he thought. He pulled his phone from his pocket. He could not linger too long over this decision, since everything would be in an uproar tomorrow.

Opening his texts, he messaged Grandmother: *I'll take the job if you'll still have me.*

Three little dots popped up a moment later indicating that she was responding.

The next question is will she have you.

I'll see you tomorrow.

Tomorrow! He texted back, and then relaxed. Tomorrow was going to be a disaster, most likely. Things would be messy, and the very fact that he had known about her"death" ahead of time would make a stint in the London office would be a wise choice, at least for a little while. He had done a few internships in the office before he had joined the military, so he was not a complete stranger to the business.

Laughter floated down the hall—Tacey's giggle, mixed with the children's. That was something Edwina would never be caught doing.

Now that more of his life was decided, he left his room and ambled down the hall to see what was going on. The three children and Tacey were playing a board game and giggling over how *Sorry!*™ was not"sorry" in the least.

"Come play with us, Miles!" the kids cheered.

"But there is only room for four, and there are already four of you." Miles protested.

"You can play with Edwina!" decided the oldest child.

"But does Edwina want that?" asked Miles.

She glanced up at him with a smile that caused him not to hear her answer right away.

"I wouldn't mind."

"Uh—well, I guess, then. What color are we?" he said, coming to sit beside her.

"Green."

"Christmas tree green!" said the middle child, wrinkling his nose.

"Do you not like Christmas trees?" Miles asked.

"They stink!"

"He only says that because they make him sneeze," stated the oldest, with a shake of her curls."He chose taxi yellow."

"And which did you choose?"

"I chose," she said, with a refined gesture placing her hands over her chest—a gesture he had seen from her mother."Christmas red. It's also the color of roses."

She's going to be a heartbreaker.

"And which did you choose?" he said, turning to the littlest, whose bright blue eyes were peeking out from underneath her messy brown hair, a smudge of chocolate on her cheeks.

"Blue!" she put in with a solemn blink.

"It is . . ." started her older sister.

"Just blue!" the youngest repeated, and touched one of her blue pieces with her sticky forefinger.

Miles grinned at Tacey."So, whose turn, is it?"

"Mine!" said the youngest, shifting to a kneeling position so she could reach a card."Five!" she said and prodded one of her blue pieces farther down the line.

"Who do you think is going to win this game?" Miles whispered to Tacey.

"I am," declared little Miss Blue Eyes.

The two older siblings exchanged peeved glances.

"I don't know, but you and I don't have even one of ours out of the gate," Tacey whispered back.

"I said I was sorry!" protested the middle child.

Tacey's laugh filled the room."Indeed, you did! I was just letting Miles know that we are on a hard-pressed battlefront and defeat may be imminent."

"Not with the right battle plan," Miles answered.

"And that would be . . . ?" Tacey asked.

"Pulling all of the right cards!"

Tacey laughed at this and shook her head."Sorry, but this is a game of chance. Not strategy."

They played a few more rounds before the butler came in and announced dinner.

"It will just be the five of you this evening; your parents messaged to say that they are wrapped up in paperwork down at the lawyer's office and that a meal is being catered in for them."

Dinner was an elegant meal of sausage rolls, chips, with a side of steamed vegetables.

"It's what the children requested," the butler explained before he left them to eat.

"How about a movie after dinner?" Miles asked a.s they dug in.

"Yes! Are we going to go out to a movie?" asked the oldest.

"No, we've got plenty of good choices right here," said Miles.

After dinner Tacey suggested that it might be more fun if they were to have a pajama party. The children agreed and changed into pajamas while Miles and Tacey changed into something less formal. Tacey snuck into one of her favorite hoodies.

Miles picked out a classic Christmas movie and they all snuggled down together on the long couch with hot cocoa, biscuits and peppermint sticks. Miles stole a glance at Tacey curled up at the other end, the littlest one falling asleep on her lap. She looked so at home. How he wanted it to be home. He wanted *them* to be a home—for *this* to be their family ten or so years from now, settling down on a frosty winter evening with hot cocoa, blankets and a Christmas movie. He was glad he had changed, his pocket where the ring had been still felt like it was burning . . . but it was now tucked away and that would have to wait.

Unexpectedly, his phone buzzed. It was a text message from Edward Seymour. *Catching a seven o'clock flight; be there around eight am tomorrow. Will text when we have a better ETA.*

It's going to be like a deck of cards tomorrow . . . unless . . .

He glanced in Tacey's direction and found she was looking at him curiously. He smiled and shook his head. After all, it wasn't something she needed to worry about *right* now, and he didn't know how to break the news to her, exactly . . . or even if he should.

He texted back. *Let's meet for breakfast.* That would let him get her out of the house and Edwina into it with the least amount of drama.

Perfect. Text me the location. Me and my wife will meet you there.

He searched the web for some nice restaurant with a private room for this encounter to take place.

Glancing over, he saw the children were all sound asleep. It had been a long day for them, and despite her nap Tacey looked like she was not very far behind them.

The movie ended just as he heard the scuffling of feet at the front door. Everyone was back from the lawyer's office. He snuck out of the living room to greet the parents.

"They are all sleeping in the living room," he whispered.

"Oh, the dears! They were so neglected today," said Aunt Flora with a sigh."We'll carry them up to their rooms and tuck them in."

Tiptoeing into the living room, Uncle Arnold and his wife scooped up the two oldest in the blankets they had fallen asleep in. Carefully Miles followed their example, untangling the youngest from Tacey's arms to carry her to bed. Tacey stirred.

"Shh," he admonished."You should go to bed, too." She nodded slightly but made no motion to move. When he had entrusted sleeping Miss Blue Eyes to her mother's care, he returned to the living room and found Tacey was still sitting there, too awake to fall back asleep, too tired to move.

He sank down on the couch across from her, it was just like their first night in New York, except this was their last night, and in London.

"Should I carry you to your room, too?"

She laughed sleepily, and her eyes met his."I don't want tomorrow to come."

"I know. Me neither."

She brushed hair out of her eyes."What are we going to do tomorrow?"

"There is someone I want you to meet. And if we go out for breakfast, I can meet Edwina at the airport and return with her; it would make for the least amount of drama."

She sighed."It would. What time for breakfast?"

"Around eight, maybe nine."

"I'll be ready."

"All right. I'll see you tomorrow, then."

"Tomorrow," she smiled.

Twenty-Five

Miles rose from the couch and exited the room. And with it went a piece of her heart.

Today—this afternoon and evening—had been everything she had ever wanted and dreamed of. She wanted all of *this*.

Is that selfish of me?

This had been everything she had imagined a family could be. It wasn't hard to imagine *them*—having a future like this. Them and three little children packed onto a couch watching Christmas movies—of course it wouldn't always be like that. Relationships took work. But of all the relationships she had in her tiny world, she wanted *this* one to work. She had had a taste of something she didn't want to lose.

But . . . who was this friend he wanted her to meet? *That seems like a strange sort of arrangement. I'll have to ask him more about it in the morning.*

She dragged herself up the stairs and crawled into the bed that was hers for the night. She curled up into a tiny ball, and tears started to trickle down her cheeks.

This day—she didn't want it to end.

She wanted to savor every moment. It had been so sweet, and tomorrow . . .

Tomorrow she would be without a family again.

She closed her eyes and tried to shut out the tears.

Oh dear God, help my heart. It's breaking into pieces! I thought this job would be easy, but I'm afraid that tomorrow I might break in pieces. I've had a taste of all that I ever hoped and dreamed of, and tomorrow I have to leave it all behind. Comfort my heart and give me strength for tomorrow. this hurts so much . . .

Twenty-Six

Her phone buzzed. Blearily, she opened up her eyes to peer at the screen.

Miles.

She slid to answer."Hello?"

"Hey? I'm sorry; did I wake you?"

"Yes," she answered, groggily.

"I am sorry Tacey, but we're scheduled to meet my *ahem* friend in about thirty minutes, and it's almost that far across town."

"Oh, no. I'm so sorry! What should I wear?"

"Whatever makes you comfortable. You don't have to worry about being classy. The more you are yourself the better, I think, in this case."

"Who is this friend?"

"I'll tell you along the way, okay?"

"I'll be down as soon as I am ready."

She rolled out of bed and pulled on her New York clothes: her favorite floral hoodie, her best pair of jeans, and her black knee-high boots. Running a brush through her hair, she pulled it back into a ponytail, and flicked on a little mascara and swiped on a liquid lip tint before dashing down the steps to meet Miles in the entryway, where he stood holding her jacket.

"No one is up yet. The sooner we are out of here . . ."

"Where are you guys going?" peeped a small voice from the balcony.

"Out; I'll be back later, okay?" Miles replied, holding his finger to his lips as he rushed Tacey out the door. The air was cool and crisp; it smelled of frost and evergreen boughs. A taxicab was waiting for them. They slipped into the back seat.

"So, who is this friend that we are meeting this morning?" Tacey asked, hesitantly.

"I've met him only briefly before. He was at the gala; you might have met him . . ."

She gave him a look.

"Or not . . ." he said, slowly clearing his throat.

"No, I didn't, other than the rush line of guests."

His lips formed a grim line.

"What are you trying to tell me, Miles Henderson?"

"I've been doing some background work on you."

"Background work on me?"

"I don't think you are—um—who you think you are."

She tilted her head."What do you mean?"

"You have a family, Tacey."

"That's impossible! If I had a family, they would have come for me by now, and not waited until I was eighteen."

"I don't think it is impossible, and I think they didn't come for you because they thought you, well, hated them. This man and his wife have flown all the way from New York to see you. That is who we are meeting for breakfast."

"My family, but . . ." She shook her head decisively."No, that is impossible. I don't have family, Miles."

"I think you do, though, of course, I don't know for sure yet." He took a deep breath."I didn't say anything before because I didn't want to get your hopes up."

She sat for several dumbfounded minutes, staring at him as this wave of information crashed over her with tidal effect.

"You mean I've had family this whole time and they've never come looking for me until now?"

"I don't know the whole story. All I know is that he sounded very eager to meet you on the phone, but like he thought you never wanted to see *them*."

"I don't understand. I don't understand at all. This hurts. This all hurts." She shook her head."Life made so much more sense before all of this. I thought I was all alone in the world, and then that gala I found that there were so many people like me, and that there were things to help them—us—that I never received; and now I am finding out I might have a *family* after all these years! Miles—I don't know if I want to meet them."

He unbuckled his seat belt and scooted over to wrap his arms around her."I am sorry," he whispered."I am so sorry."

Her stomach churned with fear; she felt like she was suffocating, and pushed him away."Why didn't you tell me all of this sooner?"

"I didn't know anything myself, really, until we were flying over here. It's come together so quickly. I didn't know *how* to tell you. I'm sorry."

She looked out the window and watched London speed by all ready for Christmas, while she—she didn't even know who she was anymore.

Twenty-Seven

ere we are!" the taxi driver said, stopping in front of a small restaurant. Miles paid the driver and then his hand touched her arm."Are you ready?"

"I don't know if I can do this, Miles."

"Let's get out of the cab and walk around the block; you might feel better with some fresh air," he said gently.

She looked up at him. Waves of emotions crashing over her from all sides. Fear swelled over her while a riptide of betrayal by Miles yanked at her. but his eyes and hands gently coaxed her from her seat, and with a nod she followed him into the brisk morning air.

She inhaled deeply and slowly released it. "I just don't know . . ."

"If you don't want to go in there, I'll drive you straight to the airport and you can fly home."

It was exactly like what she wanted to do—but coming from his lips, it sounded like an act of cowardice.

"Why haven't they wanted me before now?"

"I think they'll have a good explanation for you, if you'll talk to them. But if, at any time, you don't feel comfortable, just say the word and I'll take you home."

Home. That word, it made her heart ache. *He* was the closest thing to that word, he felt like home, she wanted him to be family. She took another deep breath of the frigid air.

"Okay, I'll give it a try. Promise you'll get me out of here?"

"I have never left a man behind, and I am not leaving you!" He whispered, stepping closer.

His words made her toes curl in her boots and she wished that was a promise he was making for longer than just this moment.

She nodded and he offered her his arm.

"I am sorry for pushing you away in the cab. You have done so much for me, and I . . ." she looked away as shame crept up her cheeks.

"It is okay, Tacey. You're dealing with a lot and you've done really well. I know this isn't easy."

"But I was churlish . . ."

A smile crept across his face."You're starting to sound like a proper little Brit."

Tacey grinned up at him and tightened her grip on his arm.

Oh, how I crave his protection and strength!

As they entered the small café, she saw another couple waiting for the waiter in front of them. The woman glanced back at them, and sudden emotion swelled in her face.

"Edward." She caught her husband's arm and tilted her head towards Tacey and Miles.

The man turned and gasped, tears springing to his eyes.

"You look just like Judith—" The words died on his lips as he looked into her eyes, and then pulled her into a hug."You look just like your mother," he whispered hoarsely.

She felt Miles squeeze her hand and release it. Letting go of Miles hand she wrapped her arms around this fatherly man.

The man pulled slowly, still holding her, as if he was afraid, she would bolt.

"Are you all right, sweetheart?" His hands cupped her face with fatherly affection.

Tears that had been filling her eyes spilled over."I don't understand." she whispered."Why are you so happy to see me? Do you actually want me?"

"They said you never wanted to see us."

She shook her head."I never even knew you existed!"

"Can I offer you a seat?" broke in a waiter.

"Henderson, party of four," answered Miles.

"Ah, yes . . . the back room! Right this way, if you please."

Tacey walked in a trance to the back room where she sank down in a seat beside Miles and across from her Uncle Edward and his wife.

"They never told you about us?" asked Edward Seymor.

"No, they said I had no one to claim me. Are you certain that we are related, and that I don't just not a look like your sister?"

"I have documents," said Uncle Edward, fumbling with his briefcase and pulling out several manilla file folders."Here is all the information. Here is your mother and father's marriage license, and a copy of your birth certificate. Um . . . here are—"

Everything seemed to stop when she saw a picture of her mother and father—and her. It was their last family photo. Tears now streamed from her eyes."I haven't seen them since—" She gathered the photo into her arms longing to hug them. The photo was the closest thing.

"Mommy! Daddy!" The words came in a sob.

Miles wrapped his arm around her, and she leaned into him, feeling as if her heart had both shattered and fallen into place, all at once.

Twenty-Eight

*M*iles held onto her gently, as if she would break. The look in her uncle's and aunt's eyes was agonized as they watched her sob in his arms.

Her uncle reached into his briefcase and pulled out a recorder. He set it on the table and pressed the red button.

"Tacey—darling," he said quietly, his hand reaching for hers across the table. She emerged from Mile's shoulder but still leaning into him, but reaching for her uncle's outstretched hand.

"I am going to show you some papers, and you need tell me if you remember them—what they mean to you. Some of them have a signature on them."

He showed her paper after paper that claimed that she, Tacey Canty,"didn't want to leave the care she was under", that she was"mentally disturbed" at the thought of leaving friends that she saw as family, and statements in her name that claimed that her mother's family had been so abusive to her mother that she had left the family.

Tacey shook her head."I don't remember any of these. I know I went through more paperwork than any of the other children, but they never told me what they were for. They just told me to sign them. if I had known anything about you . . . but that is not what they told me at all what the papers were about. They said if I didn't sign them, they would have to put me out on the street."

Her uncle winced."Did you receive any of the money we sent you?"

"Money? There was no money. They told me I was so much trouble..." She bit her lip and looked at her uncle."Was there money?"

"There was a fund with monthly allowances for clothing and food for you. We even tried to make contact with you on your eighteenth birthday, but they said you cleared out your bank account and took off with your boyfriend."

"Boyfriend? Cleared out my bank account? I didn't even know there was a bank account. And I never had a boyfriend. I was too busy. The lady kicked me out on midnight of my birthday." She closed her eyes, more tears slipping down her cheeks.

"I am so sorry, I should have hired a private investigator. There were just so many doctors and psychiatrists and other people that said you were better where you were, and then when the accusations arose that my sister was abused by our family and that is why she left, well, we almost lost our own children to the system. I stopped fighting for you for fear of what I might lose, since they were willing to take a money settlement that would provide for you. I wrongly thought I was doing the right thing. I am so sorry Tacey—I am so, so, so sorry. If I had known the truth . . . can you find it in your heart to forgive me for not doing more?"

"You wanted me?" she asked quietly.

"We did," replied her aunt, opened a manilla envelope containing all their petitions.

Tacey read them through tears. The server came in silently with a tea pot and cups then left again. Miles poured her a cup preparing it just the way she had it the day before at Grandmother's.

Thirstily Tacey sipped her cup of tea.

"Why would they do this to me?"

"They wanted the money, and I deceived myself into thinking they truly had your best interests at heart. And I see now I was wrong, so wrong, Tacey." Whispered her uncle.

"You tried for years . . ." she said under her breath in disbelief.

"We did."

"Thank you. Thank you for trying."

"I shouldn't have just *tried*. I'm a lawyer. I should have gotten you back from their clutches."

She bit her lower lip. "It helps knowing that you cared enough to try. I thought, until today that I was . . . alone. And now . . ." Words failed her as she glanced up at them.

"Come home with us," urged her uncle softly. "I know I can't make the past up to you but come home with us for Christmas—and for always."

"You want me?"

"Yes, we want you! We have always wanted you!"

Tacey couldn't hold back her sobs anymore as she stood up and walked around the table. Her uncle and aunt stood and gathered her in their arms, and the three of them hugged, weeping a mixture of sorrow and joy. Miles stood and stepped out. There was something sacred about the moment, and he felt they needed privacy. When the sounds quieted, he entered again after obtaining a glass of water for Tacey. Tears needed more than tea.

He set it on the table in front of her and she looked up at him. Then she stood and reached her arms towards him. He pulled her close.

"Thank you—thank you for giving me just what I wanted for Christmas! It is more than I could have ever imagined!"

He squeezed her tightly. "It's the least I could do."

"Thank you, Miles. You have done more for me in this past week. You are my hero."

A lump was growing in his throat. He gave her one final squeeze before slowly stepping away. "I am so glad I could help."

She smiled. Shakily she sat down again, and he sat beside her. "Shall we order some breakfast, and talk a little more about family?" asked her uncle.

"I'd—I'd like that," Tacey whispered.

The menu was perused, and items ordered, though afterwards no one really knew what they themselves had ordered. They were far too distracted to actually read what was on the menu. Fortunately, the waiter seemed to understand.

Time passed swiftly, and Miles' phone started buzzing.

Miles where are you? Edwina is already back. We will be reading the will in half an hour. How long do we need to wait for you?

He tapped back. *Sorry mom, I can be there in about half an hour.*

"I am so sorry," he said, standing up."I have to go to—." He looked at Tacey, trying to find the words to explain.

"Oh, is it that time already?"

He nodded.

"Edwina must be furious. She's probably been texting me a storm—and I left my phone back in her room." She bit her lower lip.

"It will be fine. I'll take care of everything. You'll be okay here?"

"Yes I will," she said, glancing at her aunt and uncle.

"I'd better go now . . ." he said huskily.

"I'll see you later?" she asked with wistful hope.

"Yes, you'll see me later. You can count on it."

He flagged down a taxi. Hopping into the back, he gave the address of the lawyer's office. When he arrived, he quickly made his way to the meeting room where everyone else was sitting around a large oval table. The oldest girl sat staring at the freshly-tanned real Edwina. *Well, at least she's arrived.* He took a seat and apologizing for his tardiness.

"Now, as we begin—" said the lawyer, pointing to a screen with a PowerPoint presentation of the will.

"That isn't Edwina," pronounced the oldest child, interrupting the lawyer.

"What?" said Edwina, glaring at the child.

"Edwina was wearing jeans when she left this morning, and you aren't wearing jeans."

Miles bit back a smile and stifled the laugh that was building in his chest. His hand covered his mouth, and he hoped his face wouldn't betray him as he kept his eyes averted, staring at the charts meant to describe the current stocks and bonds in trust behind the lawyer with dogged determination.

"Yeah! You don't seem like the Edwina that played with us yesterday," piped in the small boy, glowering at her.

"Of course I am the Edwina who played with you yesterday!" stammered Edwina.

"Yeah?" challenged the boy, his eyes narrowing."What game?"

"What color was I?" chirped the youngest, her expression defiant.

Edwina fumbled for words."I . . . uh . . . you were . . . oh, don't be silly!"

"Miles, *that* Edwina—" the middle child pointed"— didn't play with us yesterday, did she?"

He swallowed hard. To be asked point blank. He cringed.

Edwina was shooting daggers at him with her eyes. He was torn; so torn. Part of him wanted to roll out the grand red carpet of betrayal that Edwina had manufactured, but a small part of him wanted to save her the embarrassment that she was going to suffer if and when everyone else found out.

"Umm, this Edwina?" he fumbled musingly as he secretly texted Edwina"You owe me. You played *Sorry* . . ."

Her phone buzzed a moment later, and she looked at him in shock before turning to the children."Oh! I forgot—I played *Sorry* with you."

"What movie did you watch with us?" pressed the oldest.

"Children, really!" interjected in their mother, at last.

"She's not Edwina!" persisted the oldest.

"No, she isn't!» agreed the second.

"Not Dweena," said the third, folding her little arms for emphasis.

"I am Edwina," said Edwina."Jetlag must be messing with your minds."

"Children, now," said their mother.

"Mom!» protested the oldest."She's not our Edwina."

Just then the screen flashed a picture of Edwina in Tahiti sipping her pineapple smoothie, time stamped and dated nearly twenty fur hours old.

Then a photo of Tacey at the Gala. Then Edwina at the beach. Then Tacey and Miles leaving the passport center—Miles noticed that Tacey was smiling shyly up at him. He wondered at how he had missed it.

He ached to see Tacey.

"How dare you!" screamed Edwina, turning towards him savagely.

"Edwina! What does all of this mean?" said her father sternly.

"Me? I was helping you!" Miles protested, putting his hands up in surrender, but ready to defend himself if she lunged across the table at him.

"Yes, what does it mean, dear?" asked Grandmother, stepping into the room.

"Grandmother!" chorused the children.

The adults were too shocked to say anything.

Leaving the table, the three children clustered around and embraced her tightly."We missed you!"

"And I have missed you, too. Now I need you to sit quietly while Grandmother and all of the adults have a good long chat."

The children quietly resumed their seats and occupied themselves with the coloring sheets that the office had thought to supply them with.

"Now Edwina," said Grandmother.

"Mother!" Henry at last choked out.

"Yes, Henry, I know I played a horrible trick on you, but there was someone in the family playing a worse trick. Several actually. The good grades trick, the identical twin trick, the—"

"Grandmother!" blurted Edwina, in shock.

"I know everything, so it'd be best for you confess before I tell everyone everything."

Miles glanced at the three children. They had paused their coloring and were now staring at Edwina in synchronized judgment, and the youngest shook her head disapprovingly, as if their ages were reversed.

Miles cleared his throat. As much as he thought he had wanted to see Edwina getting this talk, he realized now he didn't really want to."How about the four of us go get some ice-cream," he suggested to the children.

There was a unanimous agreement, and taking the two youngest by the hand, they embarked into the streets of London in search of ice cream.

Twenty-Nine

Dinner was awkwardly silent, except for the children loudly talking over one another as they described their day with Miles. They had had ice cream, ridden a bus, gone through a museum, and had returned home just in time for the evening meal with everyone else. The youngest had acquired a British accent in her travels, and now did not seem to be able to speak without it, much to Miles amusement.

His phone buzzed and he looked down at the text.

Taking Tacey home on a midnight flight. Can we swing by and pick up her things?

His heart lurched.

Tacey was leaving so soon.

Of course. He texted back and gave them the address. *Let me know when you'll be here.*

Will do—about half an hour away.

Dinner had just finished when his phone buzzed again. *Here.*

Miles excused himself and went to the front door. After all, he was an American and he wasn't going to wait for the butler to answer their knock.

Besides, he needed to see Tacey.

Opening the door, their eyes met. He noted the glimmering of happy tears still shimmering in the corners of her eyes.

"Hello," he greeted, feeling a sudden dryness in his throat."Won't you come in?"

"Thank you, if you don't mind," said her uncle, and they all stepped inside.

"I'd better go get my things. Do you know if Edwina is in her room?" Tacey asked shyly.

"We just finished dinner, so I think she's still in there" Tacey bit her lip, and he sensed she didn't want to meet Edwina just now."Do you want me to go up with you? I can run interference if needed."

"I'll do that," interjected her uncle."She showed me the contract that Edwina had her sign, and if anything does come up, I'd like to have a few words for Edwina."

Miles stayed silent. From her demeanor at dinner, he could tell Edwina had been raked over the coals more than enough, and this wouldn't buoy her outlook on life at all.

Just then Edwina stepped out into the hall.

"You—" she hissed, walking viciously towards Tacey in her tappy stiletto heels."—betrayed me to the uttermost! I will—"

Miles stepped in front of Tacey to be her shield.

"You will have nothing more to do with my client—and niece," interrupted Edward Seymour, stepping forward and proffering his card."Edward Seymour, from Seymour & Seymour. You will be hearing from me on Monday regarding this matter."

Edwina looked down at the card in shock"What?"

"Your stepbrother is quite a detective. He discovered a thread that tied Tacey to my family, and we have been reunited."

"What?" her voice rising in pitch with every repetition.

By this time, the whole family had gathered behind Edwina in the hallway.

"Miles, what is going on?" asked his mother.

He turned slightly to glance at Tacey. She returned his look with a smile and stepped to his side. He resisted the urge to put his arm around her.

There was an audible gasp from most of the family.

"I told you that that wasn't our Edwina!» said the boy.

"Our 'Dwina!" said the youngest, running up to her. Tacey bent down and hugged her, tightly.

"You want to know a secret?" said Tacey wrapping her arm around her

"What?" she asked, with wide blue-eyed wonder.

"My real name is Tacey."

"Tacey? I like that better than 'Dwina. Have you been crying?"

"A little."

"Who made you sad? Was it 'Dwina?" she asked, still in her newly acquired British accent.

Tacey smiled slightly as she shook her head, and Miles could almost feel her emotional pull for the strength she needed.

His heart ached, how he wanted to give it to her. She leaned forward and kissed the little girl on her forehead."No one made me sad—these are actually happy tears."

"Happy tears?" The little girl scrunched her nose."What are those?"

Tacey laughed."You'll figure it out sometime. You'll be so happy, you'll just start crying happy tears."

The little girl squinted her blue eyes in mystification, but then nodded and seemed to accept that that was just something she couldn't grasp yet.

"I wish the real Edwina was like *our* Edwina," announced the middle child. This earned him an emphatic"Shh!» from his older sister.

"Our Edwina's name is Tacey!" clarified the youngest, moving to take Tacey's hand."Tacey, won't you stay and play a game with us?"

"Oh, I wish I could but we are going to the airport, and I'm going—home." There were tears in her voice again and Miles wished that they were alone so he could hug her.

The youngest pouted and turned back to rejoin her siblings.

Tacey straightened to her full height. Miles brushed her arm with the back of his hand, and a moment later, the back of her hand moved to be near his—it was an invitation—He took it and she leaned against him, her hand securely in his.

CHAPTER

Thirty

She took a deep breath, her hand still nestled in Miles'. As she leaned against him, she realized how much he had been her tower of strength in the past week, and she didn't want to leave him. But she was going home. He had given her something she couldn't have fathomed in a thousand years. *I just want to be alone with him, to tell him thank you for everything he has done for me . . . and for all that he's been to me and I am incredibly grateful and forever in his debt.*

The continuing conversation broke into her thoughts. "The resemblance is uncanny. But how did we miss it?" said

Edwina's stepmother, blinking at her like an owl that had been awakened at noon instead of midnight.

"You saw what you wanted to see," answered Grandmother.

Tacey smiled at the kind, elderly woman.

"However," said Grandmother, stepping forward,"I am sure we can get everything settled out of court, and whatever is wrong will be made right. Miles, why don't you introduce Tacey to the family?"

He was looking down at her—smiling. Her core fluttered with butterflies. There had been so few smiles in her life; well, so few that had been meant for her, and somehow this smile felt like everything.

"Mother, Henry, meet Tacey Canty."

"It is a pleasure to meet you," said his mother, stepping forward to shake her hand. His mother stood before them with a searching look in her eyes and a slight smile."Glad to meet you. Are you all right?"

"I am better now. Miles has done so much for me."

"Well, as shocking as this all has been, it was a privilege to have you as my daughter—even if it was just for a little while."

"Thank you," answered Tacey. She didn't know what else to say. Miles' hand tightened ever so slightly on hers, and she squeezed back.

"We need to get going if we want to catch our flight," interrupted Tacey's Aunt.

"Of course. Let me get my things."

"You mean my things?" Edwina said cattily.

"No, just my things. I brought a few of my own, like the outfit I am wearing now."

Edwina made a face at her, and she was so grateful that Miles was holding her hand.

"I'll help you," offered Miles.

She nodded. There was really nothing to help with, but . . . a few moments alone.

They walked up the stairs, hand in hand, to Edwina's room. He opened the door and stood in the hallway as she entered. Going to the corner, she picked up the duffle bag containing all her things. Slinging it over her shoulder, she returned to where he still stood.

"That's it?"

She nodded, unable to find words.

He sighed deeply."I'm going to miss you," he said quietly.

"And I you. I never did get you a Christmas present."

"I wouldn't worry about that if I were you."

"You gave me the world, though. How can I ever thank you?"

"Just be yourself," he whispered."Be Tacey Canty."

"I will."

He stepped forward, opening his arms for a hug. She stepped into it, shyly hiding her face against his shirt.

"When will I see you again?" she whispered.

"Soon," he answered.

"How soon?" she asked, looking up at him.

"Very," he said quietly."Now, let's get you back to your aunt and uncle before you miss your flight home for Christmas."

She nodded. The next few minutes went by in a blur: he took her bag, they walked the stairs, she said goodbyes to everyone, and then she was back out in the cold and stepping into the car with aunt and uncle. She was going home!

I am going home! Home at last! but I am afraid, I think I might have left my heart in London . . . or rather with someone.

Pulling out her phone, she tapped out a text to Bethany.

You'll never believe this. I am going home, for Christmas.

CHAPTER

Thirty-One

Eleven Months Later

*L*ondon is too far away, but I am *so* glad you could join us for Thanksgiving!"

"Me too! How are things going?"

"College is going well. Uncle was successful in his lawsuit; that was awful, but I am glad it is all over. Therapy has been very helpful to process, everything that has happened."

"You definitely seem happier."

Tacey sighed."I am happier. Holes in my history that were gnawing at me are finally filled. Things are not perfect, and I'll never be an Ivy League college student like my cousins, but that never was one of my dreams."

"Do you still have that dream that we, uh, talked about?"

She glanced up at him.

"We were in the jeep, and I asked, if you could be anything . . ." He let his words fade away. The Tacey that had sat, curled up, in his jeep a few months ago was so different from vibrant Tacey that stood beside him now, but at the same time, she was still the same Tacey he had been falling deeper in love with every day—even with an ocean between them.

She smiled at him. "Yes, that is still my favorite dream." Her expression changed. "You know what, there is another conversation we never finished?"

"There are other unfinished conversations?"

"Yes. Are you ever going to tell me what you want for Christmas?"

"Thanksgiving just finished, and you're already asking me about that?"

Her head rested against his arm as they strolled around her uncle's estate in Vermont.

"You said you would let me know *soon*—before last Christmas—and now it's been almost a year, and I still haven't gotten you a thing."

"You haven't? What about those lovely cufflinks? I wear them at the office almost every day."

"Those were for your birthday—not Christmas."

"But you've already gotten me something for Christmas. I saw the little package with my name on it."

"You've been snooping! Yes, that is for you, but not for Christmas. That is a Thanksgiving present."

"I didn't know people gave gifts for Thanksgiving."

"Well, Tacey Canty does—at least, when it comes to her boyfriend," she said, blushing, looking teasingly up at him."Since you haven't told me yet, I have two Christmases to shop up for: this upcoming *and* last."

"Two Christmases?"

"Yes!" she said with a laugh.

That laugh. I'll never get tired of hearing it, Tacey Canty.

"Well, since you really, really want to know, I have decided what I wanted for Christmas last year."

"What?" she said, swinging to face him, her bright eyes dancing. He observed with pleasure how much she had changed in the last eleven months. She was secure, happier, and, somehow, even prettier. He knew that her world made sense now that she knew she was wanted, had been sought for, and she had been desired—it didn't take away the pain of all that she had gone through, but it had brought her peace and joy.

"Tacey," he said, dropping onto one knee, and pulling out the ring box that had been searing a hole in his pocket since last Christmas. Opening it, he said,"All I wanted for Christmas was your heart to cherish, your hand to hold, and to be allowed love you all the rest of our lives . . . Will you marry me?"

"Yes! Miles! Yes!» she squealed with sheer delight.

He slipped the ring onto her finger.

Miles got to his feet and she hugged him tightly and resting her head against him as tears of joy slipped down her cheeks.

"This is the happiest day of my life!" she said with a happy sigh.

"Why is that?"

"While I have a finally and a home . . . I have someone who makes me feel like I've finally come *home.*"

The End

Years ago I came across Mark Twain's famous story *The Prince and the Pauper* and fell in love with all of the characters. A few years ago, I was challenged to take a classic and rewrite it in my own modern world and words.

After mulling over a pile of possibilities, *The Prince and the Pauper* and my deep love for Miles Hendon won out to be spun into this gender-swapped, Christmas fuzzies rewrite featuring a nod to one of my favorite books and times in history.

I hope you enjoyed your little adventure into this Hallmarkesque tale.

www.ingramcontent.com/pod-product-compliance
Lightning Source LLC
Chambersburg PA
CBHW030635120726
47904CB00006B/2163